PUNISHED BY KRAMPUS

PUNISHED BY KRAMPUS
A HOLIDAY MONSTER ROMANCE NOVELLA

SKYLA GRAY

CHAPTER

ONE

When Louis told me we'd be celebrating an early Christmas in his family's mountain cabin, I imagined a cozy little place in the woods. Quaint log walls, all of us gathered on a rug around the fireplace, mugs of hot cocoa, etcetera.

I should've known better. A family richer than God would never spend the holidays in a place like that. Still, when we round the bend and our destination comes into view, I swallow a gasp. The "cabin" is a steel-and-glass fortress, all sharp angles and boxy modernity, stark and intense against the winter landscape. Especially imposing with the sun sinking behind the horizon behind it.

My nerves wind tighter. I've been anxious about this weekend for months. Meeting my fiancé's family for the first time was bound to be nerve-wracking. Even more so when his family is incredibly affluent and mysterious. People say there's something sinister about the Kohler family's obscene wealth. Something supernatural, even. The rumors range from mob connections to ritualistic human sacrifice.

Of course I don't believe any of that. But wealth on that level is its own kind of magic, one I understand enough to fear. And seeing this "cabin" is yet another reminder that I'm an outsider. When I was a kid, I was lucky to get new socks for Christmas. Or an even rarer treat: having both of my parents home for the holiday, instead of away at work. The Kohlers might as well live in another world. I guess I should've known they were different when Louis told me they celebrated the holidays on December 5th, weeks early for Christmas.

"Wow," I say after a moment passes. "It's…"

"What?" Louis's lips quirk, but the smile doesn't reach his eyes. "Hideous?"

I hesitate, studying his profile. The pale angles of his face look harsh in the watery winter sunlight, and there's an intensity in his blue eyes as they focus on the road ahead. His jaw is set in a rigid line, and his fingers grip the steering wheel so tightly that his knuckles are white.

Then he glances at me and smiles, and the tension breaks.

"It's okay," he says, laughing. "I know. The place is ugly as sin."

"I mean, I wasn't gonna say it. But you said it was a *cabin*, not an *apocalypse bunker*."

"It's not a bunker. It's aboveground."

"Yeah, okay, semantics. Why does it *look* like that?"

"My grandfather built it when he immigrated here about eighty years ago. We've updated it since then, but we try to uphold his vision."

I wrinkle my nose. "And what vision is that?"

He says it like he's reciting something sacred. "We protect our own."

Unease tightens the knot in my stomach. But I try to brush it off, make a joke of it.

"And will your family be protecting you from little old me? Is that what has you so worried?" I reach over to run my fingers through his fair hair.

His wry smile is back. "Something like that."

"Hm…" I trail my fingers down the side of his neck, trace over the outline of one bicep through his knit sweater. "Do you think you need protection, Louis?"

"From you?" He huffs a laugh. "No, I don't think so."

"No?" I lean further toward him, smiling, to run my hand over his chest, walk my fingers down his torso. "You sure?"

"Diana…"

"Yes?" I breathe oh-so-innocently, fingertips reaching his belt buckle.

"We'll be there in like ten minutes."

"Is that a challenge?" I undo the buckle, reach for the button of his jeans.

"*Diana*," he snaps, his voice harsh. I recoil. "Not the time."

I slowly sink back in my seat. "I was just teasing," I mutter, as the heat in my lower belly turns into the unpleasant burn of embarrassment. "Sorry."

Louis's jaw is set again, any hint of earlier playfulness gone. "Not the time," he repeats.

I turn my gaze out toward the snowy scenery ahead. "You're right," I say. "I'm sorry."

We spend the rest of the ride in silence. I twist my fingers on my lap.

Just a few months ago, we would do things like that all the time. Quickies in the bathroom, road head, fooling around in the back of the car because we couldn't wait to get inside the apartment. You name it, we've done it.

But everything changed when Louis proposed. It's like he's become a different person entirely. He's become so stiff that he seems on the verge of shattering.

I can only hope that this weekend will fix things. I know he's been worried about me meeting his family; he craves his father's approval, especially.

As long as this goes well, everything should go back to normal. All I have to do is make a good impression... which would be a lot easier if I weren't lying about my entire life.

CHAPTER

TWO

My boots break through a crunchy layer of untouched snow as I step out of the shelter of the garage. The first breath of mountain air is a shock to my system. It's so cold it burns my lungs, and I cough, pulling my scarf over my mouth.

"Jesus," I whisper to myself. My teeth are already chattering, the tip of my nose stinging. I'm not used to this kind of chill.

Louis grabs our bags from the trunk and takes a step toward the cabin. My heart sinks as I wonder if he's going to keep ignoring me. This weekend will be even more awkward than necessary if he keeps it up. But then he moves closer, putting an arm around my shoulders. I lean into the solid warmth of his body, inhaling the pine-and-musk scent of his coat.

"Let's go warm up in the 'bunker,'" he murmurs in my ear.

He holds me against him like the last ten minutes never happened. It isn't exactly an apology, but I'm so relieved that I let it pass.

5

The cabin is built into a cliffside. The garage is tucked neatly beneath the main house, but to reach the entrance, we have to climb a steep stone staircase. I'm out of breath once we reach the top, and Louis is struggling with the bags. He unlocks the front door with an ancient-looking key, and we step into an empty, quiet mudroom. I follow Louis's lead in stomping the snow off my boots and shedding my coat and scarf. He leads me through a door and into the main part of the cabin. I expect his family to be waiting for us, but there's no one here. Only the faint sound of classical music playing from somewhere deeper inside.

It's warmer here than outside, but still surprisingly cold. I'm reluctant to relinquish my coat to Louis, but I do it anyway.

"Sorry," he says when he notices me shivering in my dress. "This place is old-fashioned. Wood stove heating. More reliable in case of a blackout, but it's hard to keep the whole place warm."

"Oh, it's no problem. I'm sure I'll get used to it," I say, and clamp my jaw shut to keep my teeth from chattering.

Louis takes my hand, and I follow him deeper inside.

Seeing this place from the outside was one thing. Inside, it is an entirely different beast, far more decadent and luxurious than the stark exterior design would suggest. It seems bigger somehow, with the open-concept layout combining the kitchen, dining, and living room into one huge, high-ceilinged space. Polished wooden floorboards and a stone fireplace lend a rustic charm, but the rest of the house is all sleek modern luxury, from the marble countertops in the kitchen to pristine leather furniture which looks like it's never been sat upon.

Yet it's also old-fashioned in odd ways, like the heating

Louis mentioned. Gold sconces line the walls with real, flickering flames within, instead of electric lighting.

There is also what appears to be a chandelier made of antlers, which gives me pause. But Louis passes by it all like it's completely normal. I suppose it is, to him. I try to follow his lead as he brings me up the spiral staircase to the second floor, down a long hallway with a dizzying amount of doors. Louis pauses at one to bring our bags in, giving me a glimpse at the gorgeous guest room we'll be staying in. We toss our phones on the bed—there's no service here anyway—and then we carry on down the hall.

A low murmur of conversation gradually grows as we approach the end of the hallway. A mix of unfamiliar voices, hard to parse as they twine with one another and the music. I have an urge to stop here, to eavesdrop, to try to get my bearings before I walk into the room.

Without looking at me, Louis reaches back to grab my hand as if sensing my urge to balk. There's nothing to do but follow as the voices grow louder, and louder...

And stop as we step into the room.

I have barely a moment to take in the room itself: a luxurious lounge with a record player, a crackling fireplace, plush leather couches, and white carpets. *Who the fuck gets white carpets?* I think, absurdly, my attention laser focused on that before I raise my eyes to see the four faces turned in our direction. My gaze darts from person to person without managing to take in the details. I search for a hint of a smile, a spark of warmth to ground myself with. But in the flickering firelight, they all appear cold and white and expressionless, as though they're carved from marble. They look at me like they can smell the poverty on me.

"Louis!" someone cries—his mother, I think—and the

spell is broken. They're all rising, laughing, reaching out to us.

I must have imagined that moment of strangeness. A trick played on me by my own imagination, an awkward half moment made into something greater. But still, unease prickles along my spine, and I hang back as Louis steps forward to greet his family.

The first to reach Louis is the woman who spoke, his mother. A pretty woman who I only know is in her 50s due to her son's age. She's tall and willowy, fair-haired and blue-eyed just like Louis, and she doesn't spare me a single glance.

Nor does Louis introduce me, for that matter, turning immediately from his mother to a man who envelops him in a bear hug. Adrian, his brother. Louis warned me about him. *Rough around the edges* were his words, which to me meant *don't be alone in a room with him.* He looks a lot like Louis but bigger, broader, louder.

The woman standing behind Adrian, hanging back from the reunion like me, must be Adrian's wife. I stalked their pictures on social media, but even her stunning candids didn't prepare me for how beautiful she is, with her long red waves of hair and a tight dress that emphasizes her tiny waist. I squinted and zoomed in on so many pictures, trying to find a wavy background that would betray her self-editing, but... wow. I guess she just looks like that, though in person it looks less modelesque and more concerning. She's the only one in the room who looks at me, and it isn't a friendly stare. More of a quick, cutting glance, one top-to-bottom scan before she looks away. Sizing me up as though I'm competition.

Then there's Louis's father. He's the last to rise from his seat—an oversized armchair set closest to the fire—and the rest of the family angles toward him without seeming to realize it. That includes Louis, whose spine stiffens as his father approaches.

I study him over Louis's shoulder. He's a tall man, even taller than his sons. His hair and beard are almost entirely gray, but if anything it only lends a stately air to his classic good looks. A silver fox, for sure, especially when he's dressed in that tailored gray suit. It makes me feel under-dressed, despite my carefully selected, designer wool dress.

The Kohler patriarch catches my eye for just a moment and then pulls Louis into a hug, thumping him on the back.

"Good to see you, Son," he says.

Louis's posture relaxes, like he's been granted approval in some way. Only *then* does he turn to me, holding a hand out. I step forward and take it, looking at him instead of the rest of the family.

"Everybody," he says, though his eyes are on mine, his encouraging smile just for me. "I'd like you to meet my fiancée, Diana."

"Pleased to meet you," I murmur, keeping my eyes downcast, as if I wasn't just judging them silently a minute ago.

Eyes crawl over my skin like the feet of a dozen creeping insects.

"I'm so glad we *finally* have a chance to meet you," his mother says. "I wish we would've had the pleasure of your company *before* the engagement, but we're so happy to have you here now."

I smile like I didn't catch the dig, or the side-eye she shot her son as she said it. "I've been so excited to meet you all after hearing so much about you."

"Oh?" Louis's brother steps in next, studying every inch

of me aside from my face. "Please, I'm dying to know what he said about me."

I accept his handshake with a wan smile. "Oh, you'll have to ask Louis. I would never betray his confidence."

Adrian's eyes finally meet mine. His grin is wide and toothy. "How very loyal of you."

The second he releases my hand from his constricting grip, I turn to his wife with a far more genuine smile. "And you must be Anna."

"Done your research, have you?" Her fingers barely graze mine. They feel almost brittle.

"What can I get you to drink?" Louis's father asks before I can muster a response. "I heard you're a whiskey drinker. I'm quite a collector myself." He steps behind the bar and gestures to a shelf of bottles. Glittering crystals containing rich amber liquid that screams wealth.

I bite the inside of my cheek, resisting the urge to glare at Louis for passing that tidbit on. I *am* a fan of whiskey, but I doubt asking for Jack Daniels on the rocks will go over well with his highbrow family. Now, my fiancé is off talking quietly with his mom, leaving me to fend for myself. "Yeah..." I say. My eyes dart over the shelf of unfamiliar bottles. I've never seen any of these, except maybe when I ogled the bottles behind locked doors at the liquor store, far out of my price range. "What do you recommend?"

My future father-in-law's lips dip slightly, like I've failed some sort of test. "Well... I'm having the thirty-four-year-old Laphroaig tonight."

The name sounds vaguely familiar. Scotch is not my usual thing, but it can't be terrible if it's expensive, right? "Sounds perfect."

He sets a small crystal glass on the counter and grabs the bottle. My palms are already sweating as I stare into the cup; even that seems too expensive to belong in my hands. He pours me a couple fingers of golden liquor and nudges it across the bar to me.

The moment I lift it to my nose, an intense smokiness hits me. I hold my breath as I take a sip.

The moment it slides down my throat, I know I've made a mistake. I blink rapidly to keep my eyes from spilling over, and suck in a breath through my nose that only intensifies the flavor. And it was *intense* to begin with. Like a mouthful of campfire ashes. Like I just took a shot of liquid smoke. I swallow again, and again, but my tongue is shriveled, my nose and throat full of soot.

Louis's father is studying me. I force a smile through the pain.

"Lovely," I croak.

He smirks. Did he give me something that tastes like straight coal on purpose? The thought makes me want to throw this glass of gnarly whiskey straight into his eyeballs, but I force myself to take a second sip. It's just as vile, and I will probably never get the taste of smoke out of my mouth. But if this is a game we're playing, I refuse to lose so easily.

Louis's father pours himself a glass of the same stuff and takes a long sip. He smacks his lips. "I'm impressed by your appreciation for it," he says. "It's a complex flavor, but I love a nice, peated Islay."

"Mm-hmm." I can't tell if he's making fun of me, but I maintain my smile and force myself to take another sip. "So... smoky." Like biting into a burned tire.

"Almost a meaty taste, right? Such an interesting flavor profile."

Ew, ew, ew. Now that I'm thinking of meat, the lingering flavor reminds me of ham, and it makes me want to gag. "Mm-hmm," I manage. I glance at Louis, silently begging him to save me, but he either doesn't notice or doesn't care.

Thankfully, his father takes mercy on me. He claps me on the shoulder, squeezes me, and says, "I should go make sure dinner is coming along. Enjoy the rest of your drink."

As he slips away, I excuse myself to the bathroom. Not that anyone is paying enough attention to me to notice. When I lock the door behind me, I let out a long sigh, relaxing for the first time since I stepped out of the car.

But a brief second's reprieve is all I give myself. Then I lean toward the mirror, scrutinizing myself for any cracks in the mask. I wipe away a smudge of mascara, reapply my lipstick, practice my smile: small, demure, not too many teeth. I smooth down the flyaways in my hair, readjust my dress, suck in my stomach and check how I look from the front, the side, the back. This dress is clingier than it seemed when I first tried it on. I'll have to be careful how much I eat. Especially since Louis's mother and sister-in-law are so thin. I wonder if they're close, if they trade diet tips. I wonder if they're whispering about me right now.

I take a breath, shake out the tension in my hands. Being too wound up won't help me. But I can't help it. I need to be perfect tonight. Not decent, not good, not great. *Perfect.* I need to perform like I've never performed before.

The lies started as a game.

My parents were both employed by a wealthy family. They worked so hard compared to the people they served, and yet they made so much less. They always looked so tired. I started pretending to be like the family they worked for as a joke, strutting around our living room using my "rich people" voice while my parents howled with laughter.

Then my parents scraped together enough money to send me to the local private school, where I stood in front of a class of rich girls who knew nothing about me, and realized I could be anyone at all. My parents said they wanted me to have a better life, so why not start crafting myself one now?

After that, I moved across the country to get a college degree, funded by a scholarship and a series of sugar daddies. Often more than one at once, each fooled by my crocodile tears about how I couldn't afford groceries. They gave me glittering jewels, designer handbags, fur coats... gifts that became part of my future costumes, just like my degree did.

Then I found more ambitious ways to bleed the rich dry. Cons and scams and blatant thefts from high-end malls and higher-end "friends." Of course no one would suspect me, because I was masquerading as someone already rich. I'd lie and swindle and pickpocket my way into free clothes and jewelry and vacations, and move on to a new city whenever people started to get suspicious.

Of course, crafting a new life meant I had to leave my old self behind. That includes my parents. My stomach drops as I think of them; the holidays always bring that loss to the surface again. But it's better for all of us this way. My parents won't get dragged into the mess of my life, and I can maintain my fake sob story that I'm an orphan who lost her parents at a young age.

All those little lies and scams have slowly snowballed, eventually bringing me to the greatest con of all: marriage.

After our first couple of dates, it was easy to understand what Louis wanted. He saw me as a wounded dove, and himself as the hero. He wanted to take care of me, to spoil me, to heal me. In return he wanted me to be soft and grateful and submissive. A princess rescued from her tower;

pretty and quiet in public, eager to get on her knees in private.

It's not much different than what any man wants: a woman who's smart, but not smarter than them. Pretty, but never proud of it. Charming without seeming like she's trying to be. Never too loud, too desperate, too *much*.

All love is a con of sorts. My performance for Louis takes a little more effort than most, but that's mostly my own fault. Because I have more to bury. More to hide. Because Louis wouldn't love the feral, ugly thing that lives in my core, my anger with its sharp claws and bared teeth.

Nobody would.

With that thought in mind, I square my shoulders and leave the bathroom. I mean to head back to Louis's side, but instead I hesitate, eyeing the other doors in the hallway. I shouldn't snoop... but I can still hear the murmur of voices in the lounge. The better I understand Louis's family, the more I can shape myself into whatever they want me to be.

The door nearest to me isn't locked. It isn't even shut. It's cracked open, just a smidge, like it's asking me to step inside. I bite my lip, glance up and down the hall, and step toward it. I use two fingers to coax the door open. It slides open easily, soundlessly, to reveal what appears to be an office. The walls are lined with bookshelves, all of them full and neatly stacked. There are a couple of leather armchairs, and a desk with an office chair behind it. The desk is polished mahogany, and I'm tempted to go search through the drawers till my gaze finds the book.

The thick, leatherbound tome sits in the center of the otherwise empty desk. The cover is blank, the spine turned away from the door so I can't see how it's labeled. Its pages are yellow with age. The con-running side of my brain screams *expensive*, but I don't think that's the reason the book catches my gaze. It's not like I'm going to hide it under my dress and steal it away, especially when I have bigger goals for this weekend.

But there's something about it... something that calls to me. Begs me to read it, even just to *touch* it. My hand is reaching out before I'm aware of what's happening, and I step forward as if pulled against my will. Whispering stirs in the back of my mind, growing louder with each step. I can't quite decipher the words, but I'm certain I will if I can only be closer...

I can't resist the pull. Even though a part of me is screaming that this is stupid, I open the book. My fingers flip through yellowed pages of their own accord. My eyes scan dates and lists of names I can't remember—other than the constant refrain of *Kohler, Kohler, Kohler*—until I reach the pages holding familiar ones.

Karl Kohler, Theodora Kohler, Adrian Kohler, Louis Kohler, Anna Kohler. The last few pages are the same. I flip to the ones before that, find one that lists *Anna Lewett* instead of *Anna Kohler.* Further back, Anna's not there at all—there are different names instead. *Mary. Lisa. Catherine.* All women's names, all crossed out. Some years there are two of them alongside the Kohler family.

My brow furrows. The names of the brothers' exes? Is this some kind of... guestbook?

Again I hear that whispering in the back of my head. This time I can understand it.

Sign the book, it says. *Give your name. Give your blood—*

The sound of voices in the hallway makes me jump, shattering whatever strange trance I was in. I shut the book and push myself against the wall so I'm not visible from the cracked-open door.

"She's hot, I'll give you that," I hear Louis's brother say as his footsteps pass by.

"It's not about that," Louis protests. A beat, and then he says, "Well, it's not *just* about that."

I roll my eyes as they chuckle.

"I mean, that is the most important thing," his brother says. "Don't get me wrong, it'd be nice if my wife were smart, but it's not that important. I need my business partners to be smart. I need my partner to *look* good."

"I'm lucky I got both," Louis says, and I smile to myself.

"Well, we'll see how it goes. You've always been picky. Hardly ever bringing girls here, and even when you do, they never come back..."

Their voices and footsteps trail away, much to my relief. I resist the urge to glance at the book again, struck by the superstitious fear I'll fall into whatever weird hold it had on me before. I need to return to the group before I'm missed.

I step out, and move the door until it's just the way I found it. This took longer than I expected; they're probably wondering where I am. I turn and walk down the hallway as quickly as I can without looking like I'm in a rush, already thinking of a dozen excuses if anyone asks.

Yet when I pass by another cracked door, I can't resist the urge to peek. Anna stands in front of a mirror, squeezing herself into a skintight gown that makes my eyes widen. I would kill to wear a dress like that. Or have a body like that. I'm practically salivating watching the silk slide over her hips, the dip of her tiny waist, the swell of her bust. Even the curve of her neck looks sensual, decorated with a string of pearls...

My gaze slides up further, and I jolt as I realize she's meeting my eyes in the mirror. Watching me watch her.

"If you're going to stand there, you might as well zip me up," she says.

She speaks to me like I'm a maid, rather than a future sister-in-law. But I just got caught staring like a creep, so I step through the doorway to obey anyway.

I try to think of an excuse as I approach her, but the canny gleam in her eye tells me that none of them would work. She sees me. More of me than I care to reveal, I suspect. Of course someone like her, so glamorous and self-assured, would see through my flimsy facade.

Standing behind her, I brush her hair to the side so it won't get caught in the zipper. I suck in a sharp breath as it reveals the skin of her back. I expected smooth porcelain perfection like the rest of her. Instead, her back is covered in raised white scars, crisscrossing all up and down her spine. What could make a mark like that? And so *many* of them? It almost looks like she was... whipped?

She snaps her fingers, and I flinch. Caught staring again.

I swallow and slowly drag the zipper up the curve of her spine. Elegant silk swallows up the sight of those angry marks like they never existed at all. Pain hidden beneath finery.

Anna picks up a comb and begins brushing out her long hair, completely ignoring my existence without so much as a *thank you*.

"Any advice for tonight?" I ask.

She meets my gaze in the mirror again rather than turning around.

"Run while you can," she says with a thin smile.

Yet her eyes hold no humor at all.

THREE

The food looks delicious, but I can hardly taste it. There's too much restless energy buzzing through my veins. I feel like I'm on a stage, spotlight shining in my eyes, hoping that I'll remember my lines.

It's nerve-wracking... and exhilarating. I've always been the type to stand too close to the edge when I'm high up, relishing that low swoop in my stomach when I look down. Sometimes I think part of me wants to fall. I imagine it would feel, at least for a moment, like I'm flying. Free.

I allow myself tiny sips of wine. Alcohol takes the edge off, and makes sure nobody gets any ideas about this being a shotgun wedding. Small bites of food, too, to make sure I don't seem like a glutton. I want to appear like I'm used to meals of this quality, like I don't regularly shove cup noodles into my mouth while watching reality TV.

The food is surprisingly hearty fare. Braised red cabbage, rich dumplings, an entire roasted goose as a centerpiece.

"We always eat traditional German food over the holidays," Louis's father says, cutting into a goose leg. The meat is shockingly red and dripping fat. He shoves a piece into his mouth and chews heartily. "Our roots are important."

"It's delicious," I say, though I've barely touched my plate. But it feels like everyone is looking at me now, so I cut myself a thin slice and chew with some appreciative noises.

"So glad you're enjoying it," Louis's mother says, though there's a hint of judgment in her eyes. I realize she's barely eating, and Anna is pushing hers around her plate in between generous gulps of wine.

I dab at the grease on my lips with my napkin. "Did you cook it yourself?" I ask. I haven't seen anyone here but the family.

Louis's brother lets out a guffaw. "As if she's ever touched a stove in her life."

His mother looks at him with pursed lips, then back at me. "Our staff were kind enough to prepare it in advance. They were up here cooking half the night, though of course we let them go home to their families afterward."

"How considerate," I say, since she seems to expect it. As if asking her staff to come up a freezing mountain, slave away in the kitchen, and drive away without enjoying any is *generous*.

His mother waves it off with a pleased little smile. She seems to take all of my praise personally, as if she has any claim to money from her husband's wallet and work done by people whose names I doubt she ever asked for.

"So what is it you do, Diana?" Louis's mother asks. "You're an art collector, is that right?"

Of course I've just taken another bite of meat. I chew as quickly as I can, one hand pressed demurely to my lips.

"Curator," I say finally, tucking hair behind my ear as I feign humbleness. "I'm an art curator. I plan and arrange exhibitions, usually working with talented up-

and-coming artists to help get their work in the spotlight."

"We met at one of her exhibitions," Louis says, taking my hand. I smile, although he's preventing me from eating. Maybe it's intentional, because it seems like his mother and sister-in-law have stopped touching their food.

"It was amazing."

"Well, it wasn't exactly my best work," I say with a theatrical little sigh. "You remember that whole fiasco..."

"Oh, please, that was hardly your fault," Louis says. He looks over at his mother when he says, "The gallery somehow managed to mix up the dates. Diana arrived with all of her artists' work ready to display and they told her they didn't have her on the schedule. Can you imagine?"

"I was just so worried for my artists," I say with a sigh. "I couldn't let all of their hard work go to waste..."

"So Diana put her foot down, really kicked up a fuss," Louis says, with a fond glance at me.

"The gallery ended up scrambling to make it work, and so the show went on."

I smile at him. We've told this story so many times, it's almost like a practiced con. As if he'd ever be savvy enough to pull one off.

"Well, I hope they compensated you for the trouble," Louis's father grumbles, stabbing into his goose.

"We reached an agreement," I say. An agreement that involved me paying the gallery nothing while walking away with my substantial "artists' fee."

"Seeing her pull everything together last-minute was incredible," Louis says, squeezing my hand. "When I saw it, I fell in love."

"Oh, stop it," I say, though my smile is genuine.

That exhibition was one of my favorite cons. Especially

since the artists were all pretentious rich fucks all too eager to pay a substantial amount to hang their terrible art in a gallery.

Even better, that con led me to Louis, a much bigger target. All it took was a few dates of playing coy, followed by the best blow job of his life, and I had the man wrapped around my finger...

"Sounds like a scam."

My eyes slide across the table to meet Anna's. She's not even pretending to eat anymore, just watching me with a surprisingly shrewd gaze.

"Pardon?" I say, forcing a smile.

"I mean, seems unlikely a gallery would just *mix up* an exhibition's dates like that," she says.

"Never underestimate the incompetence of the average man," her husband says.

Anna rolls her eyes, but then she's locked on me again. "And isn't it, like, your job to work with galleries? Didn't you vet them before arranging the exhibition?"

"I'll confess it was my first time planning a show that big," I say, tucking my hair behind my ear in feigned self-consciousness. "I don't know... maybe you're right? It didn't really occur to me that a gallery might try to take advantage of artists like that..."

The way she purses her lips at me, I don't think she's buying it.

"You forget, Anna dear, she is *awfully* young," Louis's mother contributes, managing to make it sound like an insult to both of us.

"Oh, but surely not much younger than Anna," I say, widening my eyes. She seems like the smartest person in the room; best to make an ally out of her if I can. "She's so beautiful."

"I'd hope so, given how much I pay for her Botox," Adrian says.

Anna fakes a laugh and sips her wine, looking thoroughly unimpressed by all of us, but at least she's no longer interrogating me.

The rest of dinner passes without anything of significance. I had hoped to retreat to our room afterward. It's late—almost midnight, actually—and I want to check in with Louis about how I'm doing so far. But instead of retiring, everyone rises and heads in the same direction without a word. I'm left little choice but to follow. I keep glancing at Louis, hoping he'll fill me in on what we're doing, but he's lost in a conversation with his father and brother. His mother and sister-in-law are arm in arm, conversing quietly. I trail behind them feeling forgotten.

My breath hitches as I realize where they're headed: the office that I was snooping in earlier. Louis's father holds the door open and ushers us in, one by one. As we step into the room, a formal sort of hush falls, like something important is about to happen.

Louis takes my hand and tugs me to his side, but he doesn't provide any insight into what's happening.

Everyone is weirdly silent, so I stay silent as well. My eyes find that ancient book sitting on the desk once more, and I feel the whisper of desire to touch it. I probably would give in if not for Louis's grip on my hand. And when I glance around the room, I realize everyone else is looking at the book too. And there's something strange in their gaze. Something almost hungry.

FOUR

"I see you've already noticed our most prized family heirloom," Louis's father says as he shuts the door behind him. He locks it, too, which sends alarm bells ringing in my head, but nobody else acts like it's weird. "It's the centerpiece of tonight's festivities."

I take a deep breath and try to stay calm. "Festivities? Oh, like an early Christmas tradition?" I ask, trying to keep the strain out of my voice. Something is strange here; the back of my neck won't stop prickling.

"Tonight is a more important holiday than Christmas," Louis's father says.

I glance at my fiancé, but he's either enraptured by the book or avoiding my gaze. "Louis didn't mention we were celebrating anything in particular. Other than our engagement, I mean."

"It's a very private night for our family. We hardly ever invite outsiders to join us," Louis's father says, with an approving glance at Louis. Louis doesn't hesitate to meet *his* gaze, expression brightening at his father's attention. "It's an old family tradition. It started back in Germany generations ago, and my grandfather brought it to the new world when he traveled here. It is called Krampusnacht."

A nervous giggle bubbles out of me. "As in... Krampus? Like *Krampus* Krampus?"

Louis squeezes my hand. I glance at him, expecting him to be sharing in the joke. But instead his jaw is set in a hard line, and he won't look at me.

The laughter dies in my throat. I swallow with a dry click.

"Indeed," Louis's father continues, undeterred. "And Krampus is nothing to laugh about. The tales have been watered down over generations, but the truth is still in the heart of it. Krampus rewards those he deems worthy, and punishes those who are not."

Despite the absurdity of all of this, goose bumps ripple across my skin. "Punishes them how?"

Louis's father displays his too-white teeth, but it's hard to call the expression a smile. "That depends. For minor misbehavior, he might whip them with a birch branch. For those who have seriously trespassed..." He pauses, letting a meaningful silence stretch out. The rest of the family is silent, waiting, and I lean forward slightly in anticipation. "Some, he drags straight to Hell itself, to torture and devour."

I shudder, leaning back in my chair again. "I think I prefer the cookies and gifts version of Christmas," I joke weakly.

Louis's father regards me coolly. "As I said, it is tradition. And tradition is important to my family, enough so that we brought it across the sea with us. Now that you are to become one of us, we have brought you here to join us in the way the Kohlers have spent Krampusnacht for generations."

"Oh," I say. "Well..."

Louis squeezes my hand again in what I now recognize as a warning. I snatch my fingers away. But despite my annoyance that he didn't warn me about what was happening on this trip, I don't see any way to back out now. I'm already here.

So I force a smile. "Of course, I would be honored. How are we celebrating?"

His lips twist slightly at the word *celebrating*, as though I've said something foolish, but he gives me a nod of approval. "A game," he says.

"Oh, good," I say. "I love games."

"Competitive, are you?"

"I can be," I say, glancing at Louis.

Louis looks more relaxed now, and the look he shoots back is almost playful. "She *definitely* can be."

"I'm excited to see how you fare, then," Louis's father says, crossing the room.

"It's a competition, then?" I perk up, watching him. "What are we playing?"

Louis's father reaches his desk. He pulls out an old-fashioned-looking metal key from a chain around his neck, previously hidden under his shirt. Bending down, he uses it to unlock something beneath his desk and pulls out a parcel wrapped in some kind of cloth.

"You can think of it like hide-and-seek," he says. He sets the parcel delicately, almost reverently, on his desk, and very carefully unwraps it. It's an old-fashioned fountain pen, made of dark wood and shimmering gold. "We will spend the night hiding from Krampus. Those who successfully evade him will receive a generous gift."

I shoot Louis a mischievous grin. He studies me in

return, surprisingly somber. "And what happens if we're caught?" I ask, nudging him.

"Krampus will punish you."

"Not with birch rods, I hope?" I joke, but Louis doesn't smile.

His father, however, does. "That depends on what Krampus decides you deserve."

"Hmm," I say, resisting the urge to roll my eyes. "And who will be playing the role of Krampus? You?"

His grin shifts into something sly. "No. Not me." He steps back from his desk and claps his hands twice, so loud, it startles me. "It is time to sign our names," he announces.

The rest of the family all form a line in front of the desk, including Louis. After a moment's hesitation, I rise to follow, the last in the queue.

I remember seeing those names listed on the pages earlier, but I feign ignorance.

"Sign?" I whisper to Louis, since his father is occupied, leaning down to sign first.

Louis glances over his shoulder at me. "Everyone who's playing has to write their name in the book."

"Why?"

He hesitates, and then says, "Tradition." Then he turns forward in a clear dismissal.

I bite the inside of my cheek. His father finishes signing and moves aside for the family matriarch to move into place. Next is Adrian, then Anna, then Louis. Finally, I step up to the desk. The room is painstakingly silent, anticipation thickening the air, so I resist the urge to speak. Surely they'll explain more about the rules after this weird signing ritual.

Louis holds out the pen in offering. It's heavier than I expect, and strangely warm. I'm the last one, so I feel the weight of the entire family's eyes upon me as I look down at the yellow pages of the open book.

Karl Kohler
Theodora Kohler
Adrian Kohler
Louis Kohler
Anna Kohler

I look down at the pen in my hand and bite my lip. It's probably silly, but this moment feels important, especially with everyone watching. Mine will be the only name on this page that isn't a member of the family... yet. If I sign the book next year, I suppose it will be *Diana Kohler*.

But for now, I take the pen and write:

Diana Wilson

As I finish the swoop of the final letter, something pricks my finger. I gasp, letting the pen clatter onto the desk, and see that a wicked-looking, sharp protrusion has come out of the side of the writing implement. I must have activated some hidden mechanism, and it stabbed right into the pad of my pointer finger. A drop of blood wells up and falls onto the open page, right beside my name.

It soaks into the parchment and disappears. Like the book *drank* it.

I clutch my stinging finger to my chest and whirl to face the family. "Something just—" I start, stammering.

I'm certain it's some kind of accident, until I see them all grinning at me. Even Louis is smiling, enjoying a cruel joke that I've been left out of. His father reaches over and claps Louis on the shoulder. Louis's eyes brighten at the gesture of approval.

He's not even looking at me. I'm standing here bleeding, being laughed at, and he's more concerned about getting Daddy's attention.

Heat creeps up the back of my neck and blooms in my face. My breath comes short and fast as anger climbs up in the inside of my throat, clawing for release.

"What the fuck?" I blurt out.

That gets Louis's attention. He shoots me a look, not of concern, but of disapproval. *Disdain.* Beside him, his mother's lips form a firm line of displeasure. Adrian is smirking at me, along with his wife clinging to his arm.

"Is this some kind of prank?" I ask, holding my still-bleeding finger. Goddamn, that hurts. And I've bled on my designer dress, which means I can't return it after this trip like I planned.

"Not at all." Louis's father returns his attention to me, his hand slipping off my fiancé's shoulder. "As I said, it is a game. But I encourage you to take it seriously. In merely"—he steals a glance at the grandfather clock nearby—"a few minutes' time, this year's Krampusnacht will begin."

I look around at the room, at all of their smirking faces. The sound of their laughter still rings in my ears. I bled, and they laughed. Louis won't meet my eyes. This is getting seriously creepy, and we still haven't started whatever *game* this is.

"I'm not so sure I'm in the mood to play anymore," I say.

"It's too late to back out now," Louis's father says with an unnerving smile. "You've already signed the book."

I glance over my shoulder at the yellowed page, bearing my signature and no sign of the blood that dripped on it.

My skin crawls. My gut screams that something is *wrong* here.

"As the newcomer to the game, you'll play the first hour outside," Louis's father says, and my attention snaps back to him.

I laugh, entirely certain it's a joke, until I realize no one else is smiling anymore. Instead they gaze at me with something cruel in their eyes. Again I get a glimpse of that strange *hunger*.

"Outside," I repeat flatly. "In the snow."

"Just for one hour," Louis's father says. "Then you may join the rest of us in the house to hide until sunrise."

Even in the warmth of this cabin, my skin prickles at the memory of the biting chill outside. It's the middle of the night, and it's the kind of cold that can kill, out there.

Fast on the heels of that thought comes the memory of flipping through the book. All of those crossed-out names before Anna's appeared. I glance at her; our eyes meet briefly, one of her eyebrows arching, and I recall her warning to run.

I look back at Louis's father.

"No," I say. "I'm not going out there."

Louis's father raises his eyebrows. "*No* is not an option."

I look at Louis, who avoids my gaze, and bark a mirthless laugh. "No to the whole thing," I say. "I'm done with whatever hazing ritual or prank this is. I want to go home, Louis."

Louis slowly raises his eyes to mine. "You heard him," he says. "That's not an option."

"Because I signed a stupid book?" I scowl. "No. Come on. I get it, very funny to tease the new girl, ha-ha. But that's enough."

Louis turns to look at his father. "Um... what now?"

His father's brow crinkles in disappointment. "Adrian," he says.

Louis's brother is on his feet in an instant, grinning in a vicious way that makes every hair on my body rise in alarm. "Yup."

"Just give me five minutes to talk to her," Louis says. But he doesn't intervene as his father and brother move toward me.

"No time," his father says. "It's almost midnight, we need to get her outside."

I step back, bumping into the desk that holds that awful book. "Louis?"

As Adrian steps closer, I'm struck by an urge to grab the pen; any weapon is better than no weapon at all. But that'd be an insane thing to do. Wouldn't it? He and his family would never forgive me if I turned violent in their house. It'd be so rude of me. So *low-class*.

In the moment I hesitate, Adrian grabs me by the arm. I cry out, and Louis's father grabs the other. I struggle, but I'm helpless against two men so much bigger than me as they haul me out of the room.

"Louis!" I scream, looking back at him.

My fiancé trails after us, but he doesn't try to stop his family from manhandling me. His mother and sister-in-law bow their heads together on the couch, whispering behind their hands as they watch their husbands drag me from the room.

"Wait," Louis says weakly, as I'm half carried, half dragged down the hallway in front of him. "She still doesn't understand. I need to make sure she's taking this seriously."

"She'll learn soon enough," his father says. His hands are shockingly strong, gripping me so hard I'm sure his fingers are leaving bruises on my bicep.

"Or she won't," his brother says. His grip isn't as hard, but his nails dig into my skin, pinching me in a way I'm sure is intentional.

They force me down the stairs, and the front door looms in my vision. My feet slip against the smooth hardwood floors as I try—in vain—to slow myself down.

They're actually going to throw me outside, onto the icy mountaintop.

They're going to kill me for the sake of some stupid game. For the sake of *family tradition*.

Some part of me is still holding back. Still desperate to prove that I'm *one of them*. But instinct rears its ugly head within me.

There's a fluttering panic in my chest. The fear of an animal driven into a corner. I haven't felt this way since high school, when my first con fell to pieces after someone dug into my parents. A trio of girls cornered me in the bathroom, calling out my lies and taunting me about my family.

In that moment, like this one, I can feel the world crumbling under my feet. It gives me that same sensation I imagine I'd get it I flung myself off the side of the building. That sense of falling from a great height, but for a second, I'm free. Because I realize that whatever happens next doesn't matter. Which means I can do whatever the fuck I want, for once. No more use pretending.

I do now what I did back in high school. I focus on the hand in front of my face, open my mouth, and bite until I taste blood.

Adrian yelps and releases me. I turn, teeth bared and copper on my tongue, toward Louis's father.

I catch a glimpse of Louis over his shoulder. I've always wondered what expression he would wear if he saw the real me, all of that feral anger I keep buried so deep. I've pictured him as horrified, shocked, afraid, angry. But instead he just looks... disgusted.

It makes me pause. Makes my gut twitch in instinctive self-reproach. And in that split second of hesitation, Louis's father twists both of my arms behind my back, so fast and powerful it leaves me dizzy.

"Unacceptable behavior," he says, scolding me like I'm a child.

Then he continues marching me toward the front door.

My heart sinks. Even if I got away, where was I going to run? There's nowhere to go but out into the cold. Straight to certain death.

Just before we reach the doorway, Louis jumps in front of us. New hope flutters in my chest.

"Wait," he says, holding up his hands. "I don't want to send her out like this. She doesn't understand. Let me talk to her."

Louis's father is silent for a long moment. Then he releases me. I stumble forward, and Louis catches me.

I look up at him, blinking away a blur of tears. "Thank you," I whisper.

As he cups my face, I slip a hand into his pocket.

"It's going to be okay," Louis says. "I know this is a lot. But it'll all be worth it in the morning, I promise. You just have to trust me."

I nod, eyes locked on his, as I slowly pull my clenched hand back.

"I do," I say, and knee him in the groin.

I rush past him and out the door, his car keys clutched in my fist.

After a pause to grab my coat and throw it over my shoulders, I step outside and pause again, my blind rage abating for a moment. The world outside of the house has been transformed. It's dark, and the wind howls, biting at every bit of skin left exposed by my hasty preparations. The temperature is so cold that it hurts to breathe. And snow has started to fall, forming a white barrier that makes it impossible to see more than a few feet in front of me.

My stomach sinks. I can't drive down the mountain in this. I also forgot my goddamn phone inside, I realize—not that I had any service as it is.

"Diana!"

I may be stuck here, but I'm not willing to face Louis and his family yet, so I slam the door behind me and plunge ahead. At the very least, I can hang out in the car until my vision stops spinning. Let Louis and his snobby relatives worry about me while they play their stupid game. It's petty, but the idea of ruining their fun gives me strength as I plunge ahead.

It's insane how quickly the weather has changed. The staircase is covered in fresh snow, and I can't even see the bottom. Still, I determinedly thump my way down, clinging to the railing to avoid slipping on ice. When I hear the cabin door open behind me, I hobble faster, knowing that Louis must be on my heels.

The staircase is so *long*, and perilously slippery in the weather, but I manage to reach the bottom without falling. One step onto open ground, and my boot plunges into snow up to my calf. I grunt with effort as I lift it out again to take another step forward. This one sends my foot even deeper and throws me off-balance. Gritting my teeth, I push forward—but someone grabs my arm and pulls me to a stop.

Louis. I slap his hand away as I turn to face him. His cheeks are red from the cold, his blue eyes wide and pleading. He looks beautiful right now, like a winter prince carved from ice.

"Please listen to me," he begs.

I set my jaw. "Why? So you and your family can laugh at

my expense some more during your fucked-up hazing ritual?"

"Diana, I promise you, that's not what's happening here."

"Then what? You expect me to believe that story was *real*?"

His face is grim. "Yes."

I force a bitter laugh. "I may not be as educated as you and your family, Louis, but I'm not *dumb*."

I turn away from him and resume struggling through the snow. The garage should be just a few yards away, but I can barely see a foot ahead of me in this snowstorm. I stick my hands out in front of me, feeling for the structure, but there's only empty space.

"I need you to understand that this is real," Louis shouts, still following me. "You could be in danger, Diana, if you don't take this seriously!"

"In danger from *Krampus*?" I scream into the wind, not sure if he can even hear me. "Don't be ridiculous!"

I take another step, and the world changes around me.

A hush falls, the howling of the wind turning to an abrupt silence. The snow stops pelting my face, and the last few snowflakes drift slowly to the ground and settle there. A sense of calm falls over the mountain landscape. I blink snowflakes off my eyelids and go instinctively still. Because while it is quiet, it is an eerie quiet; the quiet of a forest sensing a predator, an eye of the storm, a fear so deep you can't bring yourself to scream.

As the storm dies down to a whisper, I can see again with perfect clarity. There is a sheet of unbroken white around us, stretching out in every direction. I can't see the road anymore. The garage is... gone, somehow, as though it's been erased from existence.

Louis reaches for me, but I pull away. "Diana, we need to go inside," he says, a new urgency in his voice now. "Did you feel that? We just went through the veil. We're in Krampus's realm now."

"His *realm*?"

Louis nods. "Modern technology doesn't travel with us. It's just us, and the cabin my grandfather built for this."

It doesn't make any sense. But when I spin in a circle, still looking in vain for the garage, there is nothing but snow and forest. I pause as my eyes land on the latter. The trees wear white coats of frost, but there is something dark between the trunks.

I blink, rub my eyes. *What is that?* I think, but I am too afraid to voice it. Louis is frozen and silent behind me, but I can hear his breath, growing faster as the seconds pass.

The darkness steps out from the trees. It is huge, and it is moving toward us.

"He's coming," Louis whispers. "Inside. Now!"

"What is that?" I stumble back, nearly slip on the ice again. Louis catches me around the waist and half drags me to the steps.

"I already told you," he says. "Now *go*. We don't have time for this."

He pushes me, and I stumble up the long staircase, my head spinning. One of my boots slips on a patch of ice, and my stomach bottoms out as I tilt backward.

But two firm hands catch me.

"I've got you," Louis says.

I glance back at him to whisper a thanks, and I see the whites of his eyes, blown wide in terror. That's a kind of fear you can't fake. It's hard to wrap my mind around the idea this might be more than a prank, but after that glimpse I caught of *something* in the woods...

I swallow and rush up the steps to the front door. I grab the handle and yank, but nothing happens. I plant my feet and yank again, the metal's chill biting into my palms, my shoulders braced with the strain.

Louis is there a second later, elbowing me aside. He grabs the handle and pulls as I retreat. I look around and realize that the windows on the front of the cabin are all now shuttered by metal, turning the cabin into a true fortress.

And the door isn't budging.

"Is it jammed?" I whisper.

Louis ignores me, straining and straining, and then lets out a low growl of frustration. He bangs a fist against the door. "Hey!" he shouts. "Let me in!"

Icy fear splinters through my chest, sinks into my belly.

"Did somebody lock us out?" I ask, louder.

Louis ignores me, continuing to pound against the door with a growing intensity. "Adrian," he shouts. "I know it's you. This isn't fucking funny!"

I look over my shoulder and my blood runs cold.

"Louis," I whisper.

He continues pounding on the door and shouting, oblivious to my quiet terror.

"I swear to God, Adrian—"

"Louis," I say, louder.

"—if you don't open this door right now, I'll—"

"Louis!" I shriek, and he finally stops.

He turns and sees what I see: the hulking creature at the bottom of the steps.

CHAPTER
SIX

It's hard to make out the monster's features in the howling storm, but I catch glimpses through flurries of snow. The terrifying bulk of its broad shoulders. The fur covering it from the shoulders down. A pair of huge horns jutting out of wild dark hair.

An impossibly long red tongue, slithering over its lips and flicking the air as if tasting it.

"What the fuck is that?" I cry out, frozen in place by my fear.

Louis grabs my hands and pulls. I stumble behind him as he yanks me along the porch. When we reach the railing, he releases me, and climbs over onto the snowy bank alongside the house.

"Where are you going?" I ask, watching with my heart in my throat. On the other side of the porch is the side of the cabin, with just a few feet of space above a terrifying drop.

He turns back and gestures to me to follow, then begins to slide along the side of the building. After only a few feet, he's gone, swallowed by the blizzard.

My breath shudders in my lungs. There are so many ways this could go wrong. One poorly planted foot, and I'm over the edge. Would anybody find me before dawn? Would they even try? How long would I survive in this weather?

I don't know. But I do know that if I stay here, that *thing* will catch up to me. I would rather face the storm than whatever that was. So I grab the porch railing and swing myself over and into white nothingness.

Snow pelts my face, stinging and blinding. The worst of the wind is blocked by the cabin, yet I still can barely see. I set my back against the side of the building and shuffle along, squinting sideways in the hopes of a glimpse of Louis, but there's nothing but white in my vision.

I move painstakingly slowly. With each second in the open air, the cold seeps into me, stiffening my limbs and numbing my face. I scream Louis's name, but I can't hear it over the roar of the wind. A particularly strong gust forces my eyes shut, and I stumble right into something solid.

A strangled gasp rips out of my throat. But a moment later, an arm wraps around me. I stifle a sob, pressing my face into Louis's chest. For a second, I thought he left me out here.

He shouts something in my ear. It takes me a few tries to understand what he's saying.

"Window?"

I follow his gaze upward and just barely make out the sight of a window on the side of the cabin. This one isn't covered by metal shutters like the rest. My heart soars—then drops again. It's too high up to reach, even for Louis.

But maybe he could—

"Boost me," Louis shouts close to my ear. I blink and pull back, staring up at him. "I'll pull you up once I'm in."

I bite my lip, looking from his face to the window. It

does make the most sense. I don't have the upper-body strength to pull him to safety if I go first. This is the only way for both of us to get through the window.

So I ignore the anxious squirming in my gut and take a knee in the snow. I interlace my fingers and hold up my palms as a step for Louis. He touches my cheek with one hand—a brief thanks, I assume—before planting the heel of his boot in my palms.

I wince, arms trembling under his weight. The ice crusting the edges of his boots bites into my skin. But I hold steady as he lifts himself up. He shouts something I can't hear in the storm, and then glass rains down on me. I duck my head to avoid getting it in my eyes, and his weight lurches off-kilter. But he clings to the wall, and I steady myself.

With a low grunt of effort, Louis lifts himself up and begins to squeeze through the window. I straighten up to watch as he wriggles through the gap. My heart seizes as he pauses halfway, and I wonder if he's stuck, if it's not big enough for him to fit. A moment later he yanks his jacket, tearing it free from the jagged edges of the broken glass, and tumbles through. Inside to safety.

Yes.

A moment later his face appears in the window, and he extends a hand to me. I blink away relieved tears that sting my cheeks, reaching up toward him. But just as our fingers brush, his eyes slide away from me. The relief melts off his face, replaced by slack terror.

I follow his gaze and see a pair of red eyes approaching through the storm. Mountainous shoulders brace against the wind. The monster moves slowly but steadily, goatlike hooves confident and sure on the icy slope.

It's here. *He* is here, and his red eyes are locked on me.

Krampus.

"Louis, pull me up," I scream, stretching out on my tiptoes to reach for him. But his hand recoils.

"There's no time," he shouts.

I shriek a wordless sound of rage and fear and protest.

"Run," he says. "You have to run! I'll open the back door!"

And then his face disappears from the window, leaving me here with this thing.

The betrayal hollows out my chest. But my anger is not powerful enough to stand up to the fear sinking its teeth into me as I turn and face the huge creature again. Through the howling storm, I hear heavy metallic clanking. He steps closer, and I see the chains wrapped around one of his fists, dragging through the snow behind him.

I scream, stumbling backward. I turn to face the path ahead, to do as Louis told me and find the back door to the house, but one of my boots slips.

The edge of the cliff gives out beneath my heel. My fingertips scrape the side of the building. My stomach bottoms out.

And I tumble backward, down the icy slope.

SEVEN

For one moment, I am free-falling.

Then I hit the ground. Snow cushions my fall, and the way I tumble takes some of the bruising impact, so it doesn't hurt as much as I expect. But I keep falling, rolling and sliding, my vision a dizzying spin of gray sky and white ground. Frozen branches whip me. The air rushes out of my lungs. I'm moving too fast to stop myself, so I duck my head, cover my face, and hope.

I roll—faster, faster, terrifyingly fast, out of control. More frightening than the fall is what will wait for me at the end. The sharp drop of a cliff? Frozen trees impaling me? Or a swift end in a pile of rocks?

The fall seems to go on forever. But gradually, I realize, I am losing speed instead of gaining it. I slow... slow... and stop, face down in a snowdrift.

For a moment I lie there, frozen and battered. I suck in one painful, shallow breath, and then another. My body is too numb to tell if I'm hurt. But as I gingerly push off the ground and lift myself onto my knees, I look down at myself and don't see any blood. I flex my fingers, touch my ribs, feel my face. Nothing is obviously broken.

The slope wasn't as bad as it appeared. More of a hillside than a cliff. But as I glance over my shoulder, I realize that wasn't what I should've feared.

Krampus is heading down the hill. *Leaping,* really, powerful legs and sure-footed hooves finding rocks and outcroppings that my flailing body missed on the way down. He is coming toward me, and he is coming *fast.*

My head whips the other way as I lurch to my feet. The edge of the forest is nearby, thick clusters of snow-dusted conifers offering shelter and a potential place to hide. I step forward—and instantly my boot sinks. I grit my teeth and push forward. I am already aching and cold and tired, but I refuse to sit and wait for death to come for me.

I refuse to die here. I refuse to let Louis and his family get away with whatever fucked-up game they're playing here.

The snow isn't as deep once I reach the cover of the trees, but the undergrowth hinders me even more. I stumble, branches whipping at my face and roots tangling up my feet, like they're intentionally slowing me down. Trying to catch me, trap me, truss me up as a nice meal for that fucking thing that's following me. I hear the crash as the monster reaches the edge of the forest, branches snapping as it plows straight through. I run faster. As fast as I can, cold air burning my lungs as I gulp it down.

Then my boot catches on the edge of a rock. I swear as I stumble, and face-plant in the snow. I scramble to push myself up and dare a glance over my shoulder.

Krampus is just a few yards away. How is he so fast?

I have no breath to scream, so I just let out a tiny gasp of terror before starting to run again. But I'm slowing down—

lungs aching, legs trembling, head spinning. Adrenaline keeps me on my feet, but I'm waning.

When another root snags my ankle, I fall again. Harder this time, landing on my hands and knees. I try to push myself up, only to fall again. My body is giving out.

No.

I grab on to the nearest tree and *drag* myself up, panting for air as black spots dance in my vision. I stumble forward again, grabbing branches for support.

It's quiet, this deep in the forest. The trees keep the wind at bay. The silence would be peaceful, except that it only emphasizes the steady clomp of hooves following me. The heavy drag of metal chains through the snow.

I whimper, vision blurring with tears. I don't even know where I'm running. I'm moving *away* from the safety of the cabin rather than toward it. But what safety could I really find there, anyway? My car is missing; the front door is locked.

Louis left me.

He brought me here. He knew this would happen.

Rage breaks through the paralyzing grip of my terror.

If I die here today, nobody will ever know. Louis and his family will never pay. I will be another crossed-out name in that goddamn book. I refuse to let that happen.

I can't run anymore, so there's only one option left. As impossible as it seems, I have to fight.

My weary feet stumble to a stop, and I grab the closest tree branch off the ground. It's heavy, but adrenaline lends new strength to my limbs as I lift it. I whirl toward the hulking creature behind me—so *close* to catching me, just a few feet away now—and heft it like a weapon.

I look up at the creature, more than two feet taller than me and thick as a tree trunk, and meet his burning red gaze.

And I open my mouth and *scream*. It's not a sound of terror but a war cry ripped from my throat. The sound echoes through the quiet forest and sends birds scattering in a flapping panic.

As the sound dies down into quiet echoes, I heave for breath and stare up at the monster in front of me, finally getting a good look at him.

He is easily eight feet tall, with broad shoulders and a thick, muscular torso. His upper body is humanoid, his face disturbingly human despite the thick horns curving out of his head and his tapered goat's ears. From the waist down, he is more animal than man, covered in thick black fur and clothed only in a ragged loincloth. Instead of feet, he has a pair of black cleft hooves that move through several inches of snow as though it's nothing. Behind him, a long black tail whips, the tuft of fur at the end dragging through the snow behind him.

His eyes are the color of fire, of blood. His pupils are horizontal like a goat's, but watch me with an eerie intelligence.

I'm not sure whether to think of this monster as an animal or a man. But either way, the sight of him strikes terror deep in my gut. His intent is all too clear from what he carries. My eyes dart from the length of heavy metal chain wrapped around one of his massive fists to the birch rod held in the other.

He looks at the stick clutched in my trembling hands and he comes to a stop several feet away from me.

Then my gaze finds his mouth as his lips peel back to reveal sharp teeth. A long, forked, red tongue slides out to glide over his canines as his eerie red eyes find mine again.

"Your punishment will be worse if you fight it."

I nearly drop my stick as he speaks. His voice is

almost impossibly deep and gravelly, edged with a snarl that no human could manage, but so close to human despite it. He speaks with clear intelligence I did not expect.

He is neither man nor animal, but something else. Something worse.

A monster.

"What punishment?" I ask.

"The one you deserve. Nothing more and nothing less."

I swallow hard as fear slithers down my spine. "Who are you to decide what I deserve?"

He huffs, twin plumes forming in the cold air in front of his face. "You know who I am." He takes a step forward. I try to move back, but my knees have locked, a paralyzing fear seeping through me. "You signed my book in blood. You knew the rules."

This close, I can smell him. It is not the pungent animal stink I expected. Instead, he smells like pine and smoke, like pepper and clove. Musty and masculine and woodsy. Christmasy.

He takes another step, and I regain my senses. I swing my branch, teeth gritted with the effort as it whistles through the sparse remaining space between us.

The monster doesn't budge. Instead, his nostrils flare and he inhales deeply, audibly, his eyes locked on me.

"I smell your sin," he says, and he sounds *hungry*.

I cannot form words in my blind panic. But as he steps forward, I swing again with a scream of fear and fury, the branch heading straight toward his broad chest.

He drops the chain he carries and grabs the tree branch midair. He tightens his grip and pulls.

The force of it lifts me straight off the ground. I gasp, releasing my poor excuse for a weapon, and fall. My feet hit the icy ground awkwardly, and I fall right on my ass in front of him.

He tosses my stick aside without breaking eye contact and bends down to retrieve his chains again.

I scramble backward in the snow as he steps forward, towering over me.

"Wait," I gasp. "Please!"

He continues toward me, step by slow step, regardless of my pleas. My back hits a tree, and I cower against it, lifting one hand in front of my face, a pointless attempt at defending myself.

I'm no angel. The lies, the cons, the stealing... I won't deny that I deserve to be punished for what I've done. But surely, I'm not the only one. Louis and his family deserve a taste of punishment too. They're the ones who brought me here, who tricked me. And I *know* they've done worse. Why do they get away with it? Why do people like them *always* get away with it?

It's not fair, I want to scream. *I did everything right.*

But I've always known that the world isn't fair. It helps me justify the things I do. My lies and theft let me tip the balance of life's scales, just a little bit. Why shouldn't I take what I want, when some people are given *everything*, for nothing other than the circumstances of their birth? Why will everyone say *eat the rich* but judge me for the blood on my teeth?

"Why me?" I cry out against the wind. Tears trickle down my face and sting in the cold. I stare up into the unfeeling red eyes of the monster looming over me. "Don't you want *them*?" I stab a shaking finger in the direction of the cabin where Louis and his family are hiding, safe and sound and warm, right now. "Don't the Kohlers deserve punishment too?"

To my surprise, the creature pauses. His nostrils flare as his head turns toward the cabin I'm pointing toward. And I swear I catch emotion flitting across his monstrous features as his red eyes narrow in anger. In *frustration*.

"The Kohlers." He speaks, his voice a low rumble that sends an entirely new wave of shivers through me. "I can smell their sin from here."

My trembling finger drops. Even in a haze of panic, I know an opening when I see one. A way to manipulate this situation to my advantage.

"Then why don't you go and get them?" I urge him. "Why don't you punish *them*?"

His snarl rips through the air, and I jerk back against the tree with a gasp. He stomps one foot on the ground, dragging a hoof through the snow.

"Every year I try," he says. "Every year they hide behind their walls."

When his burning eyes turn on me again, it makes the air freeze in my lungs. But this anger isn't directed at me.

So maybe it's time to stoke the flames.

"You claim to give people what they deserve," I say. "But you've failed." I lick my chapped lips, venture a guess. "You've been failing for *years*, taking girls like me instead—"

The monster whips the birch rod against the tree just above my head, and I flinch away. He leans over me, his lip curling.

"You think you don't deserve to be punished?" His nostrils flare again as he inhales my scent. "You stink of sin."

"As much as they do?" I ask, forcing the words out even though my voice shakes. My hands curl into fists at my sides. "That can't be true."

"They are out of my reach." He raises the rod again, his expression going cold. "My job is to punish those I can. And I have a sinner in front of me."

"No!" I refuse to give in now. "Please, I— What if I—" I pause, sucking in a breath. "What if I can help you get them?"

Krampus goes still above me, the birch rod frozen midair. "You? Help me?" He sneers as if the thought is laughable.

"Yes." I lift my chin and force myself to meet his eyes, even as I tremble. "I can help you get to them."

EIGHT

Krampus studies me. He sniffs the air again, and I have the chilling sense that he's scenting more than just my fear.

"How?" he asks.

"I can get into the house," I say. "Or... I can get them out of it."

For a moment, he just stares at me. Then he shifts his weight. I instinctively brace myself for a blow. Yet instead of striking, he hefts his chains over his shoulder to free up one hand, and extends it to me in offering.

His hand is huge and very, very warm. He lifts me to my feet so quickly and easily that I gasp, my knees weak. He holds on to me until I'm steady, and then releases my hand.

"This doesn't mean I will let you go," he says. "I punish all who deserve it."

I swallow hard. I never expected I'd be able to walk away from this, no matter what happens. All of my lies, my greed. The people I've used up and left behind. I don't expect mercy after all that I've done... But seeing the

Kohlers punished before my inevitable end will have to be enough to satisfy me. "I'm not trying to escape."

"Then why are you doing it?" His eyes narrow as he gazes at me. His nostrils flare again, scenting.

How much can he smell? Will he sense a lie? It doesn't matter right now; I can be honest about what I want out of this.

I lift my chin. "Revenge."

The monster grins, sharp teeth glinting in the light.

My heart thumps in my ears as I approach the cabin's back door.

I've been out here for at least an hour now, probably longer. I can't feel my face, or my fingers, or even the toes shoved into my snow boots. It's the kind of cold that makes my bones ache. When I *do* feel anything, it's usually a twinge of pain; my body is battered after falling down that hill and crashing through the forest, so the numbness is probably a blessing.

There's a fire in my chest that keeps me going despite the loss of feeling in my extremities. A spark of anger that only burns brighter as I approach the house. Yet I know I have to bury it for now. Krampus and I have a plan, and it requires patience.

I wipe my nose, take a deep breath of painfully chilly air, and slam my fist against the back door.

"Louis!" I shout. "It's Diana! Please, open up! Let me in!"

I don't know if he can hear me above the howling wind. Even if he can, I'm not sure he'll let me inside. But I have to try. So I yell and plead and wail until my throat is sore and my tears are freezing on my cheeks, and then I keep going, banging away with my fists when my voice fails.

I'm on the verge of giving up when I hear a metallic sound, and look up to see a narrow slot on the door slide open. A pair of familiar eyes check left, right, and behind me—and I'm glad that I asked Krampus to hide nearby until I found a way to let him inside.

The slot slams closed again, and there's the click of the deadbolt unlocking, the swish of a metal chain. I plaster on a look of teary relief, and the door swings open. Warmth spills out from the cabin, but instead of being a relief it stings my frost-coated skin. I flinch away, wobbling on unsteady legs.

Louis throws his arms around me and pulls me into the cabin before slamming the door shut behind me. I stiffen up, hands bracing on his chest in preparation to shove him away. But instead I find myself leaning into his warmth, pressing my face into his chest, letting him hold me up.

"Diana, oh my God. Are you okay?" Louis reaches over me to lock the door. He cradles my face, tilts my chin up so he can look me in the eyes. His are glittering with unshed tears, relief etched in every inch of his expression. "Did Krampus catch you?"

I swallow back anger as I remember that he was complicit in this. He knew exactly what he was bringing me into, and didn't give me so much as a warning. He left me out there. The fact I survived is due only to my own resourcefulness.

"No," I say. "I got away."

The surprise in his face kindles my rage anew. I do my best to suppress it. I can't let him know yet. Not until I get my revenge.

"How?" he demands.

"I... I don't know. I slipped and fell down the slope, and then I ran and ran and..."

"Okay," he says. "I mean... I'm glad." He squeezes my shoulders, lowers his voice. "But, listen. It'll be easier if you just tell my dad that Krampus caught you."

I search his face. "Why?"

"Because..." He hesitates. "There's more than one reason we do this. It's a test for people who are marrying into our family."

"A test," I repeat slowly, trying to understand.

"Yeah. Because Krampus only punishes you as much as you deserve. If you survive meeting him, that means you aren't secretly some terrible asshole trying to take advantage of our family. You don't have any serious secrets to hide."

I lower my eyes, afraid I won't be able to hide the flash of fury in them. *A fucking purity test.* As if *they* are so innocent.

Louis squeezes my shoulders again. "But next year we'll be married, and you'll never have to do this again."

I force a small smile, slowly raising my gaze once I'm sure I can hide the disgust on my face. "Your dad said you do this every year, though?"

"We do. But you'll be inside with us next year, not out in the cold. And Krampus never catches us here. That's why it's built like this." He gestures to the shutters over the windows, the locks on the door. "You were right from the start. It *is* a bunker, built just for this purpose."

"But..." I shake my head, wordless. "*Why?*"

"Because if we evade him till morning, we get a reward. That's the deal."

"What reward?" I ask. But I already have a suspicion. All of those rumors online about his family's wealth... the whisperings of shady deals, of dark secrets... maybe they weren't far from the truth.

Louis only smiles, and pulls me into another embrace. "Let's get you warmed up," he says. "My family is waiting."

He gives me little choice, pulling me by the hand toward the family room. But as I glance back at the door, I remember my promise to Krampus, and vow to find a way. One way or another, this family is going to pay.

NINE

L ow conversation drifts out of the family room as we approach. Christmas music plays quietly, underlaid by the crackle of the fire and the clink of ice. Louis's mother laughs a practiced, charming laugh.

Anger sizzles in my chest. I was out in the cold at the mercy of a monster, dead for all they knew. And all the while, the family was sitting in here *celebrating*.

As Louis leads me into the room, the conversation goes quiet. I raise my eyes from the carpet to glance around at each of them. They all wear matching expressions of surprise—except for Louis's father, who wears a sly smile.

His mother glances at the clock. "An hour already?" She's not trying to hide her disappointment.

Louis's fingers remain entwined with mine. "She received her punishment," he says. "She passed the test."

He's standing by my side like I wished he would all day. Little does he know it's too late.

His father lifts his glass in my direction. "Very good," he says, his eyes locked with mine. "A glass of whiskey for our newest member of the family, then."

~

As soon as it seems like I can get away with it, I excuse myself. I suppress the urge to pull away as Louis presses his lips to my cheek before I head to our room.

In the attached bathroom, I pick the sticks and leaves out of my hair and drag a comb through the wild waves. I wipe off my smeared eyeliner and reapply it. But when I stare at my reflection, I immediately tear up.

I'm a mess. This whole situation is just so fucked.

I jump at the creak of a floorboard behind me, and whirl around to see Louis standing in the doorway. He stares at me, eyes big and brown and puppylike.

"I'm so glad you're okay, Diana," he whispers.

Anger rises like bile in the back of my throat. For a moment, I'm struck by the desire to scream at him, to hit him, to pull his hair and sink my teeth into his skin. I want to see him hurt and scared, like he's hurt and scared me today.

But I swallow the impulse back, along with all of my angry words. I need him to believe that everything is okay until I get an opportunity to *really* get my revenge.

"It's—" I start to say, but then my voice breaks. My lower lip wobbles.

Louis steps closer and pulls me against him. I ball my hands into fists and cry into his chest.

"Shh," he says. "It's okay. Here, sit down."

He settles me on the edge of the bathtub and grabs a washcloth. He runs it under warm water and then kneels in front of me, gently using it to clean the grit off my knees from where I fell in the forest. I wince at the sting, and he murmurs sympathetically. He brushes his lips over the scrape on my knee, massages my calf as he slides the wash-cloth over me.

Louis has always liked me best when I'm broken. I'm not surprised when he tosses the washcloth behind me and settles between my legs again, pressing his mouth to the inside of my knee, and then my thigh. His pale eyes flick up to meet mine, and I force my expression into the closest thing to fondness I can fake.

"I'm sorry," he murmurs, breath ghosting against my skin. He lays his cheek against my thigh, gazing up at me. "I'm so sorry. This was the only way we could be together. But... I knew you'd be clever enough to find a way through." He kisses the pale skin of my thigh again, his lips lingering, his breath warm. "I knew nothing would happen, even if he caught you."

My mind flashes to the scars on Anna's back.

"What do you mean?" I ask.

"You're too gentle. Too good. What could he possibly punish you for?"

I bite back a laugh. Feign a grateful smile.

As I gaze down at the man I was willing to spend the rest of my life with, I realize he doesn't know me at all.

Yet as he continues to murmur apologies and kiss his way up between my legs, I don't push him away. I lift my hips to help him slide my panties down, and open my thighs to welcome him between them again. I fist my hand in his hair and pull him closer, pretending not to notice when he winces at my roughness.

I lean back, one ankle hooked around his back, and stare up at the bathroom ceiling as he shows me how *sorry* he is with his tongue. He's more enthusiastic than usual. Maybe it's because he truly wants to make it up to me. Or he just prefers me like this—helpless and pliable, at his mercy.

I wonder if it turned him on, imagining me running for my life through the snow. Begging on my knees in front of that monster.

As I shut my eyes, I imagine Louis in my place. Louis stumbling through the trees, falling to his knees. Pleading for his life in front of Krampus. Crying out as the birch rods crack against his back.

My breath quickens. I pull him tighter against me, legs shaking.

I imagine him sobbing, crawling, groveling in front of me. Imagine my fingers wrapped around a birch rod. Lifting it to strike him again...

I come hard with my fingers twisting in his hair and that image held firmly in my mind.

It's good he doesn't know me. It means he'll never see my plan coming.

TEN

Afterward, Louis helps me into fresh clothes, pressing kisses to my shoulder as he zips up the back of my dress. My skin crawls at his touch, but I let him take care of me because I know it will make him feel good, and because I don't want him to realize how angry I am until it's too late.

He puts an arm around my waist and pulls me back against his chest, resting his chin on the top of my head. "We should get back to my family," he murmurs. "I don't want to be impolite."

Impolite. I almost laugh at the word. This man helped his family throw me out into the cold for a monster to ravage, yet he's expecting me to stick to the rules of etiquette.

"You're right, we should," I say mildly. "But... could I have just a few minutes alone first? I'm still... processing."

"Of course," he says. "You want me to stay with you?"

"No, no. Go be with your family. Please."

I send him off with a kiss, and listen to his steps

heading for the lounge where the rest of them are presumably still gathered. Then I put on my coat and creep down the stairs and straight to the back door.

I reach for the lock, my fingertips grazing the cool metal. But then I hesitate. Is this really the right thing to do? I'm safe inside now. I could hide in here and leave Krampus out in the cold to rage, and there's nothing he could do about it.

As far as Louis and his family are concerned, I've passed the test. I'll be accepted as one of them. I got what I wanted. Didn't I?

"Where do you think you're going?"

My blood runs cold at the familiar voice. I resist the urge to yank back my hand like a guilty child caught with a hand in the cookie jar. Instead, I school my expression into neutrality before turning to face Louis's brother.

"Surely you're not so eager to be out in the cold again," Adrian says, with that god-awful, ever-present smirk on his face. I remember the way he manhandled me earlier, his fingers squeezing me in places they shouldn't have lingered even as he dragged me out into the cold. My hand clenches at my side, but I tuck it behind my back and plaster on a smile.

"This is all... a lot to process," I say, as sweetly as I can manage. "I was thinking about getting some fresh air."

He snorts. "Some fresh air? In a blizzard? You expect me to believe that?"

My smile goes rigid. He's right, it's a terrible excuse. He's drunk, but not drunk enough to believe it, and his eyes are narrowed on me. He can't possibly suspect what I'm really up to, but he's gleaned that I'm hiding something.

Little does he know, I'm hiding *many* things. So I suppose I'll have to sacrifice a small truth.

"Okay. You've caught me." My hand dives into the pocket of my coat. I hold up my packet of cigarettes with an embarrassed grimace. "What I really need is a smoke."

He laughs. "Disgusting," he says. "Didn't expect a girl like you to have a filthy habit like that."

I grate at being called a *girl*, and the fact that his eyes linger on my cleavage as he calls me *filthy*. My coat is on but unbuttoned, and I resist the urge to cover myself. As repulsive as Adrian is, it gives me an angle to work with. "That's funny," I say. "You didn't strike me as a man put off by a little filth."

His gaze darts up to meet mine, and his eyes widen at my flirtatious look before his expression settles into a pleased and unsurprised sort of smugness. Like he was expecting this all the while, and just waiting for me to prove him right.

Gag.

"I'm not," he says. "Though it's been a while since I..." He glances at the pack of cigarettes, then again at my face. "Indulged."

"Oh? What a shame." I flick open the pack, grab a cigarette. "Perhaps you should join me, then." I hold it out to him in offering. Giving him an excuse to step closer, which he does. His fingers graze mine as he takes the cigarette, and his face comes close enough that I can smell the whiskey on his breath.

"We're really not supposed to go outside tonight," he murmurs, watching my lips.

"Do you always do what you're told, Adrian?" I ask softly, teasing. I pull my lower lip between my teeth.

He hesitates. I flick a strand of hair behind my back, drawing his attention back to my cleavage. "I suppose they won't notice we're gone if we're quick about it."

"I suppose you're right," I whisper.
He reaches behind me and clicks the lock open.
Grinning, I turn and step outside into the snow.

ELEVEN

Adrian follows me like I've got a hook in his lip.

"Don't go too far," he says, loudly to be heard over the wind, casting an uneasy glance at the nearby trees.

I'm eyeing the forest too, but I can't find the mountainous monster I'm looking for. "Well, you wouldn't want anyone to spy our *filthy* habit from the windows, would you?" I ask, continuing to head deeper into the blizzard.

"I guess not..." He glances over his shoulder, doubt creeping into his tone.

"Let's just go around the side of the cabin here," I suggest, and tug one strap of my dress down on my shoulder. My coat is still unbuttoned, and it's fucking cold, but sacrifices must be made. When Adrian looks back at me, his eyes drink in the exposed skin, and he forgets his hesitation and follows me.

The side of the building provides shelter from the wind, and I quickly put a cigarette between my lips and light it in a cupped hand. When Adrian steps over alongside me, I press it between his lips. He takes a drag, and I snatch it back and place it in my own mouth with a half smile.

He coughs as he exhales. I take an effortless drag and blow it out the side of my mouth.

"Thought you were a smoker," I say.

He licks his lips. "I never said that."

I raise my brows in mock surprise. "Are you suggesting... there was another reason you wanted to come outside with me?"

He smirks, leaning in, but I step back. He reaches for me, and I step back again, smiling in between puffs of my cigarette.

Smoking was mostly an excuse to get outside, but damn, it *does* feel good to have a cig after everything I've dealt with today—and everything I intend to do.

Adrian's smirk is beginning to disappear. "Don't play coy now."

I bat my eyelashes at him and blow smoke in his face. "But I'm so very good at it!"

He lunges for me, and I dart back, laughing. Closer to the forest, though he doesn't seem to notice. Yet... when I turn to glance over my shoulder and scan the trees, there's still no sign of Krampus.

Doubt worms into me like a splinter under my skin. What if he's too slow? What if he's not coming at all? What if...

While I'm wondering, a hand closes around my forearm and yanks me forward.

"Got you," Adrian says triumphantly. He pulls me against his chest so hard, I gasp. While I'm trying to figure out how I want to play this, he grabs the cigarette out of my hand and flicks it into the snow.

I don't like the look in his eyes. He went from playful to

angry faster than I expected. I freeze, unsure how to navigate the situation. And before I can speak or react, he slides his free hand up my side and squeezes my breast through the skintight fabric of my dress.

Instinct kicks in. I slap him across the face.

He releases me, staggering back with an expression of almost comical surprise. "What the hell was that?"

Well, shit. The jig is officially up. "I was just messing around," I say lamely. "Let's... let's go back inside." Krampus still isn't here, and I'm starting to shiver. Maybe this was a mistake.

But Adrian gives me a grim smile. "I guess you like things rough, huh? Should've known." He takes a step closer. I step back, but it no longer feels like a game, or at least not one that I'm in control of. "A girl like you is way too much for my little brother to handle."

"Adrian, I was just playing," I say, more firmly. "I'm not going to cheat with my brother-in-law. Come on."

"You need a real man to put you in your place," he says, like I didn't speak at all.

Shit. I may have to run. But I'm not too eager to go into the forest again, especially because Adrian will doubtlessly lock me out here. I glance behind him, assessing the distance to the door we left unlocked... and then I go still.

A smile slowly spreads across my face.

"Hey, Adrian?" I prompt.

"If you think you're weaseling out of this, you're wrong."

I roll my eyes. "Look behind you."

He looks like he's about to speak again, but then he stops himself. I wonder if some survival instinct is finally breaking through the haze of alcohol, or if he hears the crunch of snow beneath a hoof, or feels the huff of hot breath on the back of his neck.

Either way, it's satisfying to watch his eyes grow as he slowly turns around to face the monster behind him.

Krampus towers over him, birch rods in hand, prepared to dole out punishment.

~

WHEN ADRIAN TENSES in preparation to run, I expect to witness a chase like the one I lived through. Instead, he only manages one staggering step before Krampus draws back a massive hand and slams it into the side of Adrian's head.

He doesn't even have time to scream. He just collapses in the snow.

My heart hammers as I watch Krampus bend down and wrap a length of heavy chains around the man's neck. Mingled anticipation and fear make my chest tight. I'm dizzy all of a sudden. Excited to see Krampus deal out his brutal brand of justice... and realizing that the monster was going easy on me earlier. He could've taken me down much sooner. He could've hurt me very badly, if he wanted to.

And he still might. But back in the forest, he must've been playing with me. When he pulls the chain taut and yanks a half-conscious Adrian to his feet, there's nothing playful in his manner at all.

Adrian chokes, hands scrabbling at the metal chains constricting him. His boots just barely scrape the ground.

"Confess your sins," Krampus says, his voice deadly serious.

Adrian's mouth gapes like a fish. His lips form words I can't decipher.

Krampus grunts in frustration and lowers him, loosening the chains just slightly.

Adrian sucks in a breath. Then he shrieks at the top of his lungs.

"Help me!" he screams. "*Dad! Mom!*"

I laugh despite myself. Krampus darts a disapproving look in my direction before yanking the chains tight again, cutting off Adrian's childlike screaming.

Krampus's expression is impassive, but his tail swishes, betraying his impatience. "Fine, then," he says. "I will name your sins, if you are too cowardly to do so yourself." He leans in, nostrils flaring as he drags in a deep breath. Adrian's eyes bulge in terror.

Krampus grimaces as if tasting something rotten. "You reek of lust," he says. "And envy, sloth, greed... all seven. But lust most of all." He sniffs again, and growls low in his throat. "Adultery. Covetousness. Rape."

A chill slides down my spine that has nothing to do with the blizzard around us. I wonder how far he would have gone if Krampus had not showed up... but as I touch the bruises forming on my wrist, I suspect I already know the answer.

"Will you confess now?" Krampus asks. "What have you to say for yourself?"

He loosens the chains again.

Adrian sucks in a deep breath, lets loose a hacking, wet cough. I expect him to scream again, but there's a glazed look in his eye that has replaced his former terror. His lips twitch into a manic smile as he looks up at Krampus.

"Go fuck yourself," he says.

Krampus doesn't say a word. He just yanks the chain tight and lifts Adrian completely off the ground. His boots kick in the air, fingers scraping at the metal cutting off his airflow. His eyes bulge and his face turns red.

Krampus pulls tighter. The muscles in his thick arms swell with effort.

I watch in silence, heart hammering in my ears. Though it isn't fear I feel, not precisely. I'm not sure how to name the sensation surging in my veins, but I know I can't take my eyes off the sight.

Adrian's face goes purple. His struggles weaken. His arms fall limp at his sides and his eyes roll back in his head.

I swallow past a dry mouth. Is Krampus really going to kill him? I thought he'd whip him, hurt him, but I didn't expect an execution. Yet... after the crimes Krampus named... do I blame him?

I keep my mouth shut.

Krampus yanks harder. Harder. Veins throbbing, muscles all through his torso clenched with effort. The metal digs into the darkening skin at the edges of Adrian's neck. There's a sharp *crack*, and his head snaps to the side.

I gasp, taking an inadvertent step back. But I still don't look away—and Krampus still doesn't release the chain clenched in his fists.

Instead, with a mighty roar, he yanks even harder. With a wet tear, the chains tear right through Adrian's neck. His head goes flying. Blood sprays out of him, splattering all over me. Some gets into my open mouth when I gape, and I stumble back, sputtering.

I wipe a hand over my face, trying to scrub myself clean. When I lower it, I see that Adrian's gaping, severed head has rolled to a stop in the snow in front of me.

I scream.

TWELVE

I don't stop screaming until I run out of air. Then I press the back of a trembling hand to my mouth, smothering a final whimper.

Krampus lets Adrian's body slump to the ground and kneels. He grabs a handful of snow and carefully, patiently, cleans the blood off his chains. He didn't react at all to my scream. He barely reacts to the death itself, except that he seems... more relaxed. His shoulders have slumped slightly, and his breath comes easier. When he straightens up and turns to me, even his eyes seem less red; some of the manic gleam is gone from them. He isn't in a blind rage, but appears calmer and more in control than he's ever been. Like he's... satisfied.

That keeps my feet planted instead of running. For the moment, at least, he seems sated. And despite the blood all over me and the headless corpse nearby, I feel safer with Krampus than I did with Adrian.

"You didn't tell me you were going to kill him," I say.

"I told you I was going to give him what he deserved."

I study him, but there's no hint of remorse on Krampus's beastlike face. Of course not. This is who he is. *What he is.* He was made to punish, to hurt, to kill.

I can't let myself forget that. Nor can I expect him to be merciful to me, in the end.

I stare at Adrian's headless body until my stomach churns. My hands weren't the ones that killed him, but I'm still responsible. And even though I try to think of the sins Krampus listed, of the scars on Anna's back and all those names crossed out in the book before hers appeared, I can't fight the pit of guilt in my stomach.

Someone is dead because of me.

I've done a lot of terrible things in my life, I've lied and stolen and used people, but I've never killed anyone before.

I look down at my trembling, bloody hands, clench them into fists, and raise my gaze to Krampus again. My guilt will have to wait. My punishment is coming before the night is through, anyway—a thought that, oddly enough, steadies my emotions. I'll pay my dues later. "What's next?" I ask.

The corners of Krampus's lips rise. But then a gust of wind swirls through the snow around me. I brace my shoulders, and Krampus pauses, sniffing. A chill goes through me as I realize the wind has carried my scent to him.

"Your smell," he murmurs. His tail flicks, new tension bracing his shoulders.

I hug myself, both against the cold air and the reminder of what awaits me at the end of this. "I know. But the rest of the family first—"

"It's getting worse," he finishes, silencing me.

"Worse?" I repeat.

"Your sins have grown more severe."

I follow his gaze to Adrian's corpse and swallow hard as I understand. Krampus just killed him, and I... I helped. I deceived Adrian and led him to his death. A new addition to the list of things I deserve to be punished for. How many sins will it take until I, too, deserve death? Have I already crossed that line?

If I haven't, this path will probably lead me there. Can I carry on with the knowledge that I'm making things worse for myself? With the knowledge that Krampus might kill the rest of the Kohlers, too?

Will he kill *Louis*?

I falter at the thought. I don't know if I ever really loved Louis, but I was willing to spend my life with him. I did care for him. I still do, in part, despite his betrayal.

But at the end of the day, it isn't me deciding his fate.

I look up at Krampus to find him studying me with those piercing red eyes. "I understand," I say. "I know revenge will have a price. I'm willing to pay it."

He dips his chin in a nod. But he's still staring at me, pupils fixated on my face, chest rising and falling with deep breaths as he continues to breathe in my scent.

"You are... distracting," he says.

I'm not sure what to say to that. Nor how to deal with the fact his attention makes heat bloom in my lower belly despite the cold all around me. The way he looks at me, it's almost like...

I swallow. "Let's go inside before someone realizes we're missing."

THE BACK DOOR is still unlocked. I let out the breath I was holding as the door slides open, revealing the warm and inviting interior of the cabin. I step inside and hold the door open for Krampus to follow me, placing a finger to my lips.

He hesitates on the threshold, his expression unreadable, and then plants one hoof on the nice hardwood floor. He has to duck to fit through the doorway.

I shut and lock the door behind us. It'll slow down anyone looking for a quick escape route.

When I turn back to Krampus, he's standing frozen just a few feet inside the door, gazing around at the cabin interior. He's been dreaming of this moment for decades, I realize. Generations of the Kohler family have hidden from him here. Now, he's finally infiltrated their little fortress, with my help.

He glances over his shoulder at me. His expression is difficult to read, but he inclines his head in a small, grateful nod.

I return it, lips quirking into a smile. I'm about to speak, to ask him what comes next, when a voice calls out.

"Adrian?"

I freeze at the sound of Anna's impatient voice calling. My eyes dart to Krampus, but he's looking in her direction rather than at me. His pupils are dilating, his nostrils flaring as he sniffs the air.

"Wait," I call out, before I can think better of it. "We're coming, just one second!"

The clack of her heels grows faster. "Adrian, if you're fucking your brother's fiancée, I swear to God—"

I rush to intercept her. She rounds the corner just as I'm about to, and we collide and fall in a tangle of limbs. She swears at me furiously.

"Anna, go back upstairs!"

"Try telling me what to do one more time, I *dare* you," she snarls. Then she pauses. She stares at me with growing horror, and I realize belatedly that I'm still covered in her husband's blood.

A dark shadow falls over us. We both pause, and look up to see Krampus looming.

Anna goes very pale. She sees the blood coating his fur. Coating *my* hands. I'm sure she notices, too, that her husband is nowhere to be found.

I slowly climb to my feet, shoulders braced in anticipation of a meltdown. A scream that will bring the rest of the family running, or else send them fleeing to safety. But Anna just seems... frozen. She stays on her knees on the floor, hands curled into fists in her lap, eyes wide. The only movement is the rapid rise and fall of her chest, breasts straining against the confines of her tight dress.

She doesn't move. Not even as Krampus leans down and takes a deep, audible sniff.

"I remember you," he says. He slowly circles around her, pausing to scent the air another couple of times. "I remember the smell of your sin. Your silence as I whipped you."

At first I think Anna is in complete panic mode. But at Krampus's words, it shifts to a different picture: a woman on her knees in the snow, straight-backed and silent and *proud*, even in the face of potential death.

And I'm suddenly remembering those raised scars on Anna's back, and the way she intentionally let me see them. I remember her telling me to run. It wasn't much of a warning, but it was more than anyone else in this family gave me.

"Let her go," I blurt out, before I can stop myself.

Both of their eyes dart toward me. It's almost comical how well their expressions match, both full of affronted fury.

"I don't need your help," Anna hisses.

At the same time Krampus says, "You do not command me."

"She tried to warn me," I say, heedless of their anger. I step forward, my eyes locked on Krampus. "She tried to help. She doesn't deserve to die."

Krampus takes a step toward me, teeth baring in a snarl that renders his face monstrous. "I am the one who decides what you mortals deserve," he rumbles. "I am the one who weighs your sins and deals your punishment."

I swallow hard but stand my ground, refusing to back down. If I keep his attention focused on me, then Anna has a chance to run back upstairs. She'll probably warn the rest of the family about what's happening and make my plan for the night a whole lot harder. Still, I can't bring myself to let an innocent woman suffer for my own selfish reasons.

I can see out of the corner of my eye that she slowly lifts herself to her feet. Krampus is facing me, his back to her. She has a chance to go.

But she doesn't. She stays where she is. And when I falter, Krampus's shaggy head swings back toward her.

THIRTEEN

Anna lifts her chin, looking Krampus in the eye despite the way he towers over her. Her spine is ramrod straight, uncowed in the face of a monster who has already left her permanently scarred.

"I will take what I deserve," she whispers.

Krampus nods the slightest bit. He sniffs again, his fingers running over his birch rod, which must have left those marks on her back last year when she joined the family.

"Your husband's transgressions..." he says slowly.

Anna tenses. I tense, too, watching them. I don't plan on interfering again, and... maybe Anna does deserve to be punished, if she was complicit in Adrian's crimes.

But Krampus lowers the rod to his side. "...are not yours to shoulder," he says.

I stare at him, and then at her. "You didn't know, did you?"

She blinks, her gaze sliding to me. "That Adrian was an asshole? It was pretty hard to miss."

"That he was a *rapist*."

Her mouth falls open. "*What?* I knew— I knew he had *affairs*, but—" The color is draining from her face. She turns fully to me. "Oh. My God. I thought— Did he hurt you?"

I hug myself. "He didn't get the chance."

Krampus lets out a low, frustrated growl, and our attention snaps back to him.

"Your sins are minor," he says, jerking his chin at Anna. "I have greater prey to hunt tonight. Go."

Anna blinks at him. Her hands slowly unfurl at her sides. "I..." She sucks in a breath. "Really?"

"Yes." Krampus snorts, paws at the floor with one hoof, leaving a scrape against the polished hardwood. "Go, now."

To my shock, Anna smiles—at the same time as her eyes fill with tears. "Thank you," she whispers, and retreats back down the hallway with small, wavering steps.

My brow furrows as I step to Krampus's side. I watch her leave with a strange mixture of emotions tugging at my gut. Relief, confusion, and a flare of heat that might be... jealousy?

I didn't understand how or why she could stand in front of Krampus, willing to take her punishment. But... then I imagine how beautiful, how *freeing*, it would be to hear that she doesn't deserve to be punished.

When Krampus turns his red eyes toward me, I know that I won't be receiving that same mercy tonight. But nor do I deserve it, especially now that there's blood on my hands.

We can't all be innocents.

I lead Krampus to the stairwell. For a moment I stay, listening, but there's no sign of commotion. Anna must not have told anyone we're here. Krampus stays at the foot of the staircase while I ensure nobody is nearby to see us coming, and then follows me upstairs. He grimaces as his hooves slip on the hardwood.

"So what's the best way to do this?" I whisper, peering up at him once we're in the upstairs hallway, tucked around a corner from the lounge. Krampus keeps looking around, shaking his head as if in agitation, looking some more. Distracted. I lay my hand on his arm, and he twitches, head jerking toward me. "Is something wrong?"

He pauses, breathes in through gritted teeth. "The smell." His head rises and his nose flares—then his tongue darts out too, flicking at the air like a snake. His pupils blow wide.

He always talks about smelling sin. I can only imagine how much it must pervade the air in this cabin. It must taint every surface, seeping into the walls like the pungent odor of cigarette smoke. Generations of a family who have evaded him, time and time again, within these very walls. And three of them are here now, down the hallway. Ripe for the picking.

"I know," I say, trying to soothe him and keep his attention on me. "We're so close. But we need a plan. Do you want me to try to separate them? I could see if I could bring one of them to my room..." I nibble my lip, trying to think of possibilities. Louis, at least, will be easily convinced to follow me. There's a queasy stirring in my stomach at the thought of leading him to his possible death, but I push it aside. I've already committed to this plan; there's no point in questioning it. Just like my cons, the only way through is forward. Backing down isn't an option.

"They'll assume Adrian and Anna are together, and I'm in my room, but if anyone else goes missing, they'll notice it," I say, thinking aloud. "And they'll definitely hear someone being punished in the house, but maybe I could tie them up while you go after the others, or…"

"No," Krampus says, interrupting me.

I blink at him. "No? To which part?"

He jerks his arm away from me. "All of it."

"What do you mean? Why? I can help—"

"No," he snaps, again, louder. We both pause, tense as we wait to see if anyone in the cabin heard it, but only the continued sound of Christmas music comes from the lounge ahead. "I do not need your help any further," he says, more quietly but no less harsh.

I huff out an incredulous laugh. "You don't need my help? You wouldn't even be here if not for me."

"And thus you have played your part."

I'm surprised at the strength of the anger that rises inside of me. Maybe he thinks I'll be content to step aside and let him do the dirty work, but that's the last thing I want. "This is my revenge, too."

He shakes his head. "I am already not sure if you will survive your punishment," he says, flat and unemotional. "You cannot risk doing more."

I stare down at my boots. One of them is stained with blood, I notice with a sort of detached horror. I think that might be a bit of brain, too. I'll probably have to throw it out.

"Do you understand?" Krampus asks. "You must stay out of it. Leave the rest to me."

My fists clench. I slowly lift my eyes to meet his steely gaze again, take a breath, and—

"Diana? Is that you?"

Krampus's head whips toward the sound of Louis's voice down the hallway. His grip on his birch rod tightens with an audible creak of wood.

A shiver goes down my spine. After what I just witnessed outside—blood on the snow, Adrian's head landing at my feet—there is no question what lengths Krampus will go to with his *punishments.* I may be about to witness the slaughter of the Kohler family. A slaughter that wouldn't be possible without my cooperation.

Yet Krampus will only kill them if that's what their sins merit.

My pulse pounds, but it's not trepidation making my hands tremble. It's anticipation.

"Let's give them what they deserve," I whisper. I shrug off my bloodstained coat, revealing the still-pristine dress beneath. Can't have my appearance ruining the element of surprise.

Krampus glances at me. He shakes his head, jaw clenched, in warning.

"Diana?" Louis calls again, closer than before.

"Yes, darling, I'm coming," I answer, and walk down the hallway toward him. Krampus reaches out as if to stop me —but his hand drops, and I walk by. I wait until Louis's head disappears into the lounge again, and gesture for him to follow. With every step, I know I am only getting myself in deeper, but I don't see any other option at this point. I've started this and I'll see it through to the end, no matter the consequences.

And so, I lead Krampus straight to my fiancé and his family. They're still in the sitting room, with their whiskey and their smiles, thinking they're safe. Cheerful Christmas music drowns out the heavy clop of Krampus's hooves approaching.

I stop just outside of the doorway, plaster on my sweetest smile, and walk into the room. Calmly, slowly, head up. Far more confident than I was the first time I walked into this room earlier tonight.

There's no sign of Anna, and it's clear she didn't warn the rest of them about what's coming. Louis's expression brightens as he looks at me, but my eyes slide past him to my would-be future in-laws. Louis's mother barely spares me a glance as she sips her wine, her lipstick leaving smears of red along the rim of the glass. His father, though, gives me a curious, almost assessing once-over. As if he sees my newfound confidence and is wondering what has changed. He looks past me to the door—and I brace, wondering when Krampus will enter, but after a moment Karl looks back at me.

"I don't suppose you've seen my other son around?" he asks.

Is he suspicious of me already? Could he be so smart? I wet my lips as I slide onto the couch beside Louis, resisting the urge to watch the doorway.

"We didn't cross paths," I say. "Why?"

"He said he was going to look for you."

He exchanges a glance with his wife, who presses her lips into a thin line before taking another large sip of her wine.

I almost laugh as I realize what they're thinking. Louis's father doesn't suspect that I've teamed up with their enemy. He suspects that I cheated on my fiancé with his other son. Once again, they are underestimating me. I can't wait to make them regret it.

"How strange," I murmur, brushing my hair over my shoulder as I lift it in an affected shrug. "You'd think we would've crossed paths."

I'm eager to play into the idea, for some amusement if

nothing else. I'm not sure what Krampus is waiting for, but maybe he wants me to separate them. Maybe I can get one of them to go look for Adrian and Anna...

But as Karl looks back at me, his eyes narrow. "Is your hair wet?"

Shit, did I miss a bit of blood? I glance down, holding up a strand for inspection, but it's just melting snow.

"Did you go outside?" he demands before I have a chance to answer.

I cross one leg over the other. "I needed a smoke," I say, since I don't care what these people think of me anymore. "Should I have done it inside?"

Karl stands up, his face creasing with anger. "Louis," he barks, "into the panic room with your mother and your fiancée."

Theodora rises immediately, clutching her wine glass.

Louis stands up as well, but his face is marked with confusion rather than concern. "I'm sure that's not necessary, Dad..."

"I locked the door behind me," I say, staying in my seat.

"Forgive me if I decide to verify that myself." Karl heads for the door, glancing back at us. "Panic room, and stay there until I get back. *Now*."

As he heads toward the hallway, a number of things happen at once.

Louis reaches for my hand, even as he voices an apology.

His mother heads toward the desk, presumably to open the panic room.

And Louis's father steps into the doorway—and directly into the broad, bare chest that has stepped forward to fill the space.

He stumbles back and looks up into the stony face of Krampus staring down at him.

Then the screaming starts.

FOURTEEN

For all of his flaws, Karl Kohler is a brave man. Caught between his family and a hulking monster that has been hunting them for generations, he plants his feet and spreads his arms. Willing to be their shield and their sacrifice.

Theodora, too, surprises me. She's screaming, high and constant and panicky, but she scrambles toward the desk instead of cowering.

Unfortunately, the same cannot be said for their son. Louis runs. He doesn't even glance back to see if I'm following. He staggers toward the back of the room, pawing at the bookshelf there, sending leatherbound books and priceless trinkets crashing to the floorboards.

I watch all of this from the couch, still frozen in my seat, half in shock and half in entertained delight as I watch the chaos play out.

A moment later, Louis's mother finds the button she's looking for, and the shelves swing inward with a *click*, revealing a hidden passageway. Louis is gone the second he has a chance, sprinting into the darkness. I catch a glimpse of him disappearing downward, his boots echoing on descending metal steps.

I expect his mother to follow. But instead she reaches under the desk and straightens up with a shotgun in her hands. As Krampus slams his birch rods into the side of Karl's head to send him sprawling to the floor, the barrel of the gun swings toward him.

I shout and lurch across the room toward Theodora. She barely seems to register me—her eyes sliding over me the same way they have all night—as she plants the butt of the gun against her shoulder, squares herself, and fires.

I'm so close to the shot that I can *feel* it vibrating through my bones. A high-pitched ringing drowns out all other sounds. I tackle Theodora to the floor, even though in the back of my mind I know it's too late, I'm too late, the gun has already gone off and Krampus is too large of a target for her to miss. Even as I straddle her torso and pin her to the floor, I know it's pointless.

What a fucking fool I am. This whole time I've lauded the fact that Louis's mother is underestimating me, but I underestimated her right back.

She slams the butt of her shotgun into my cheekbone as if to drive that point home.

I grunt in pain as my skull rattles. We end up in an awkward tug-of-war with the gun, neither of us strong enough to fully overpower the other. But I'm on top, and I know how to fight dirty. So instead of trying to get the weapon out of her hands, I grab both ends of it and shove it down toward her neck. I press it closer, closer, till it's flush against the skin of her neck, and then I keep pressing. Her eyes bulge as the gun's body cuts off her airflow. Her manicured nails scrabble at it, one caught on the trigger.

Then a hand seizes me by the hair and yanks me off of

her. Louis's father stands over me, breathing hard as he stares at me.

"What in God's name has gotten into you?" he asks. "We're not the enemy here."

I twist in his grip, trying to get a look at Krampus, but he doesn't let me. Yet if he's here, and Krampus isn't, then… that gunshot must have taken him down.

My stomach twists. It can't be real. It can't be over just like that.

I twist and writhe in Karl's grip, clawing at him as he continues holding me by the hair. Theodora sits up on the floor, pressing a hand to her neck as she catches her breath. Her other hand still grips the shotgun, and she looks like she'd love to aim it at me.

"She's hysterical," Louis's father says in a tone that brooks no argument. "I suspected she was lying about being caught by Krampus earlier, but I let it slide."

Louis's mother glowers at me. She knows better than to excuse a woman's actions as *hysteria*, I can see it in her eyes, but she seems reluctant to argue with her husband. Her finger twitches toward the shotgun's trigger, then draws away as she lets out a reluctant sigh.

"Well, I'm not going to be locked up in the panic room when she's in a state like this," she says with a sniff. She struggles to her feet, using the shotgun barrel as a crutch.

I consider grabbing it, but I know it'll only earn me more pain. I'm on my knees, unarmed and outnumbered. I've lost.

"We'll lock her out here," Louis's father says.

"Wonderful idea, dear."

They share a tender smile while I continue struggling in Karl's grip. It turns my stomach, the idea that they get to share a heartwarming moment over Krampus's corpse and my helpless pain. I hate that they've won. People like them *always* win.

When Karl tosses me to the floor, I don't even try to get up. I just lie there and breathe, face pressed to the cool wood, as I listen to the Kohlers retreat into their panic room. The hidden door shuts closed behind them with a dull click.

Christmas music is still playing from the record player, mocking me. I'm going to smash that goddamn thing.

I finally drag myself up to my knees to do exactly that, but then my gaze finds Krampus sprawled out on the hardwood. Blood pools beneath him, spreading slowly across the lounge floor. His eyes stare, sightless, at the ceiling. His chest has been ripped open by the shotgun blast.

My mouth falls open and tears gather in my eyes. I didn't believe it, not really; I was still clinging to some fairy-tale hope. But now...

I crawl across the floor and kneel at his side, bending down to press my forehead to his cheek. It's still warm. Hot, even.

"I'm sorry," I cry to his corpse. "I should've... I should've done more, I..."

I collapse into helpless, racking sobs. Distantly, I realize it's foolish to cry over this monster. Theodora probably saved my life with that shot, too. Krampus was never my friend, just a temporary ally until we achieved our shared goal.

He was terrifying. Focused. Determined to deal out justice, no matter what it cost him.

He was... everything I wish I was.

My fists clench in my lap. I shut my eyes against the flood of tears, head bowing, shoulders shaking as I cry.

I've always known that the world isn't fair. I saw my

lies, my theft, my cons, as a way of righting the balance, just a little bit. But my justice was selfish and small. Krampus was the real deal. He could have changed things in a way I never even dared to dream of.

He deserved better.

And I... I deserve to be punished. I was starting to crave it, even. There is a hollow ache in my chest at the thought that I will never receive whatever he had in store for me. I will never know what I deserved in his eyes. If my sins merit death, or if I deserve absolution. Now I'll be forced to carry the question—and the guilt—for the rest of my sorry life.

I sob harder at the thought. "It isn't fair," I whisper. Life isn't fair. The truth I've always known. But for a moment, when I was with Krampus, it felt possible that it might not be true. "It isn't fair, it isn't fair..."

A massive hand closes around my wrist. I scream, trying to jerk away, but it holds me steady.

"Crying over me, little sinner?" a low, familiar rumble asks.

FIFTEEN

I raise a shaky hand to wipe away my tears and see something impossible: Krampus's fiery eyes locked on me. *Alive.* My gaze darts down to the fatal wound on his chest, but it's no longer as gruesome as it was before. As I watch, it slowly seals itself up, fresh skin covering the gaping hole as though it never existed.

Krampus sits up, his hand still gripping my wrist. "You thought such a weapon could kill me?"

I choke out a half sob, half laugh. "Well, you looked real fucking dead for a minute there."

He cocks his head. "Yet still you tried to fight them."

I open my mouth and shut it again. It's true; there was no real reason for me to tackle Theodora after she had already shot Krampus. There was nothing to gain and everything to lose. I could've forced out some crocodile tears and followed them into the safe room.

The thought didn't even occur to me, when I thought Krampus was gone.

"I told you I'm all in," I say. "I meant it. I want..." I

almost say *revenge*, but I'm not sure it feels right anymore. "Justice."

Krampus rises to his feet, lifting me with him before releasing his hold on me. "Where did the Kohlers go?"

I turn toward the bookshelf, which looks like a normal wall now that it's closed. "The panic room."

We wordlessly go to work, trying to find a way in. The tears on my face slowly dry, and so does the blood on the floor. That goddamn Christmas music is still playing, but I leave it on because it's better than having silence between us. I feel awkward, and vulnerable, after he saw how I cried for him. Something has shifted between us.

But there's no time to figure it out. We have bigger concerns. Like this goddamn panic room.

Now that it's shut, there's no sign of a way in. Even after Krampus and I tear all of the books off the shelf, there's no hidden button or lever that we can find, not even a raised groove that we can pry open. It's easy to find the button that opened the passageway on the underside of the desk, but nothing happens when I press it. It must be locked from inside now.

I straighten up from where I kneel under the desk, look at Krampus, and shake my head.

"I don't know how to get in. I'm sorry."

Krampus slams a fist against the desk. I jump back, startled by the noise and the violence of it. He's never lost his temper like this before—always seemed cool and collected even when he was wringing the life out of Adrian—but now his ears are pinned back, his red eyes radiating fury.

"I was so close," he says through gritted teeth. He slams his fist again, and a cup of pens topples off the edge and spills across the floor. I press my back against the wall, eyeing him warily. "Closer than I'd ever been. They were here. They were *right here*. And I lost my opportunity, all because... all because of..."

Because of me? I wonder when he doesn't finish. But no, that's not right. I didn't do anything wrong. If anything, it was because...

Because he wouldn't let me help like I wanted to. If he had let me separate them before he stepped into the room, they wouldn't have had a chance to do this. There's no way in hell that I'm going to say that out loud, though, when he's in this mood. But when I raise my gaze to his face and find him staring at me, I suspect he's thinking the same thing already.

With a bellow that shakes the walls, Krampus swipes an arm across the desk and sends everything clattering to the floor. I flinch at the sound—shockingly loud, shockingly *animal* as it tears free from his throat. One hand covering my mouth, I watch in shock as he stomps around the room, flinging books and crushing broken glass beneath his hooves. He grabs the record player—still spewing Christmas music—and heaves it across the room, sending it crashing against the wall. "O Holy Night" dies off mid-song, and leaves behind a vast and echoing silence.

Krampus stops in the middle of the room, shoulders slumped and chest heaving. Frustration is written in every tense muscle.

I've never seen him like this. But I still don't feel afraid of him. Instead, I feel sympathetic. I'm frustrated too. It must be a thousand times worse for him, after the years he's waited for this, only to be foiled at the last moment. Every breath must bring with it the smell of sin, reminding him of how close he was.

Instead of an urge to run, I feel an urge to try to lift his burden. But how can I help? Unless...

I take a hesitant step toward him, and then another, slowly crossing the room to reach his side. He doesn't move as I stand on my tiptoes and reach with trembling hands to clasp his face. Only then does he raise his head to look at me.

"You need to clear your head," I say.

He huffs, as if to suggest *easier said than done.*

"Take the edge off."

His expression remains stony, but his ears perk.

"Use me," I whisper. I lick my lips, still holding his gaze. "Punish me... please."

His gaze. "You don't know what you're asking for. After what we did to Adrian..."

"I don't mean the full punishment," I say. My mouth is dry. "Just a little. To take the edge off, like I said."

His eyes widen, pupils growing. He goes very still.

"Would that help?" I ask, my voice barely a whisper.

He slowly removes my hand from his face. He doesn't need to answer; I can see the need written plainly on his monstrous features.

There must be something seriously wrong with me, because part of me thrills at his response. I shouldn't be excited at the thought that he wants to punish me. I certainly shouldn't be turned on at the idea of being punished.

But as Krampus lifts his birch rod and slaps it against one of his palms, the shiver that goes through me is not entirely fear. I slowly sink to my knees and bow my head, surrendering myself to him. My breath quickens as he circles around behind me, even more so when the sound of his hooves stops. I brace with my hands on my knees, fingers digging into the fabric, and shut my eyes.

Crack.

The first strike of the rod across my shoulders brings more shock than pain. I gasp, eyes flying open again. Before I can fully process the feeling, the rod comes down again.

Crack.

This one hurts. Tears spring to my eyes, and I dig my teeth into my lower lip to keep quiet.

Crack.

A muffled groan comes from my lips as this blow lands on stinging, already-tender flesh. But there is another feeling beneath the pain, something surging and growing that I can't name.

Crack.

I cry out as my sore flesh throbs. But there is an answering ache between my thighs. I spread them, sinking lower on the floorboards.

Crack.

There is pain, yes. But on the other side of pain is relief. Sweet surrender. A part of me craves the next blow even as the hurt deepens.

Crack.

"Yes," I cry out, shocking myself—and him, judging from the way he pauses. I freeze, shame heating my chest. A moment later, Krampus steps up beside me. A rough hand grabs my face from behind and lifts it, forcing me to look up at him towering above me. Tears blur my vision, so it is impossible to read his expression.

"We should move on," he says. His voice sounds rougher than normal, deep and gravelly in a way that goes straight to the damp heat between my legs. "Before I lose control."

I release a shaky breath. "I... I can take more."

He chuckles darkly. "And you will, little sinner. Later." His other hand grabs me around the waist, and he lifts me to my feet. His grip lingers for a moment longer as my trembling legs steady beneath me. Then he releases me and walks away without looking back.

I wipe my eyes and take a moment to gather myself. What the hell was that? I'm a mess, tears streaming down my face and back aching. But when I reach back to assess the damage, I find raised welts but no blood.

He was holding back. I'm sure he was. This really was just a taste of the justice he intends to deal.

I should not be excited at the prospect of more. I swallow back my emotions, ignore the lingering ache between my thighs, and follow Krampus to continue seeking our revenge.

SIXTEEN

Krampus and I spend a good hour exploring the cabin, searching for any hidden spaces or other entrances to the panic room. On the first floor directly beneath the lounge is a tucked-away laundry room, noticeably smaller than the room sitting atop it. There's not enough space for a panic room to sit behind the wall, but there must be the stairwell I caught a glimpse of, leading further down.

I suspect from the start that we won't find another way in; there clearly was a reason that the family chose to gather in that room, and Louis was always eager to return to it after a couple of minutes away.

Louis. That coward. I can't believe he left me, *again*. If I had any qualms about what I'm doing to him and his family, that action erased them.

As I explore the cabin and consider its layout, I become more and more certain that the panic room must be some-where below the first floor, in a hidden basement. There's nowhere else that would make sense. But I can't find any way to get down there, not even in the form of a laundry or garbage chute. Because of course they wouldn't dirty their panic room with such things, knowing they might be forced to retreat there for the night.

"We could light the cabin on fire," I suggest, when we're done exploring other options. We're still in the laundry room. I lean against a wall, wincing as I put pressure on my abused back. It hurts, but… there's something satisfying in the hurt, like a pleasant soreness after being thoroughly fucked.

Krampus glances at me, and I press my thighs together, wondering if he can smell my arousal like he smells my sin. He looks so disapproving…

"The panic room is likely fireproof," he says. Because of course, he's thinking about my arson plan, *not* whether or not I'm turned on right now. I should do the same.

"Right," I say. "And the smoke will rise, so that's no good…" I pause, nibbling my lip. Fire won't work, but there's something there that pings my instincts. Fire. Smoke. Air… "They still need air," I say, realizing. I push away from the wall, wincing again, and search around the room with renewed vigor. "There have to be vents."

Krampus watches me. "Vents," he repeats, skeptical.

"Yes! They'll still need airflow, and so…" I push aside a hamper and find an air intake low on the wall. "Here's one. I just need a screwdriver, or…"

Krampus reaches down and rips the metal covering right off the wall.

"Or that works." I crouch and squint at the dark, dusty passageway. I see it turn downward at the end, which means this probably leads to the basement. "Perfect."

Krampus's skepticism has only increased. "Tell me you do not intend to climb into that thing."

"What? Hell, no." I laugh, straightening up. "It's way

too small. Here, follow me, I need to find some cleaning supplies."

KRAMPUS STILL SEEMS BAFFLED, but at least he trusts me enough to follow as I search the house. Soon, we return to the air vent with a huge bottle of bleach and an equally huge bottle of vinegar. Simple, innocent cleaning supplies that just about everybody has on hand... and when combined, they create—

"Chlorine gas," I explain with a smile. "It's nasty. Smells terrible, and feels even more terrible when you breathe it in. Burning, coughing, breathing problems... and, well, death, if you breathe in too much. And the best part?" I eye the vent again. "It's heavier than air, so it will sink right down into the basement. They'll have to either stay there and suffocate to death, or run for the exit."

For a moment, Krampus is silent. I wonder if he's decided I'm even more wicked than he thought, that maybe he's made a mistake working with me. But when I look up at him, he grins at me with a proud sort of viciousness.

"I would never have thought to do such a thing," he says. "You are brilliant."

I flush at the praise, and busy myself with the supplies. Nobody has ever seen the real me before, the one who thinks of plans like this, and I doubt most people would call me *brilliant* for it. They'd be far more likely to call me *deranged, sick, crazy.*

"Well, I haven't exactly done this before," I say. "Hopefully it works in practice... and I don't make too much and kill them right away."

"It will work," Krampus says.

I nod, assured by his confidence. "Okay. Are you ready?"

"Yes."

I splash an eye-watering amount of vinegar into the bucket I brought. Then, holding my breath and turning my head away, I add the bleach, and pour the mixture into the vent before retreating. Krampus scoops me off my feet and carries me out of the room, his ears flat against his head.

"Terrible smell," he says through gritted teeth, taking me all the way to the back door so we can step out into the fresh air.

I gulp it down despite the cold, and wipe my stinging eyes as he sets me on my feet. "Hopefully worse for them."

Then we quiet down, listening. We aren't sure exactly where they'll emerge from.

It doesn't take long. Soon, we hear the metallic groan of doors bursting open nearby, followed by a riot of coughing and swearing. They're closer than I expected; there must be a tunnel leading outside. Krampus and I share a grim smile before following the sound toward the snow-covered hill on the side of the cabin.

The metal hatch opens from a clever hiding place in a cluster of rocks disguised by the landscape and covered in a layer of snow. I would've struggled to find this tunnel even if I knew where to look. But my chlorine gas has success-fully chased the rabbits out of their hole. There's a faint yellow tinge in the air around the open doors, and Louis and his parents are scattered across the hillside nearby, choking and retching.

My fiancé is on his knees in the snow, gasping for air in between racking coughs. His parents have managed to stay on their feet, but they both look disoriented, eyes streaming and legs unsteady.

By the time they see us, we're almost on top of them.

Louis's father holds the gun now, and Krampus goes straight for him. But I home in on his mother instead. She's armed as well—with a fucking crossbow, of all things—and I'm not going to underestimate her again. As she blinks tears from her eyes and levels the crossbow at me, I know the feeling is mutual.

I sprint at her, bare-handed, and tackle her to the snow.

For a second, I wonder how I managed to get her without getting shot. Then I notice the bolt sticking through my upper arm.

"You crazy bitch!" I shriek.

We grapple with the crossbow between us, just like we did with the gun. But instead of trying to fight a losing battle, she tosses it aside and jabs her long fingernails toward my eyes. Soon, we dissolve into a clawing, biting, hair-pulling catfight.

Behind us, I can hear Krampus and Karl struggling in the snow. The gun goes off once, and it takes all of my willpower not to turn and see how my monster fares.

"Louis!" Theodora screams as I pin her down in the snow. "Help me!"

I spare a glance sideways. Will Louis come to help her? Will he attack me to save his mother? I catch a glimpse of him staggering to his feet in the snow, head whipping between where Krampus fights his father and where I struggle with his mother. Then he takes a step back, and another. He shakes his head wordlessly, turns tail, and runs into the forest.

Once a coward, always a coward. But this time it works in my favor.

Fingernails slash across my cheekbone as I'm distracted, and I turn my attention back to Theodora.

"My husband and son don't see you for what you are,"

she pants as I try to keep her sharp nails at bay. Blood drips down my cheek, splattering onto her cheek. "They think you're just a foolish pretty girl. But you're not. You're *dangerous*. And I do not tolerate threats to my family."

In response, I spit in her eye. She shrieks, writhing beneath me.

"You dirty little *animal*," she screams. "We never should've allowed you inside! We should've left you out in the cold!"

"Yeah, you probably should've," I say, and slap her across the face.

We roll through the snow, tearing at each other with teeth and claws like we're both feral beasts. I'm younger and stronger than her, but she has a wiry strength of her own, and I'm already wounded. When she grabs the end of the crossbow bolt and shoves it further into my shoulder, I black out for a second. When I come to, she's on top of me with her hands around my neck. The tendons in her thin body stand out as she throttles me with a shocking strength. I struggle against her, but she has me pinned and helpless, and my nails aren't sharp enough to do as much damage as hers.

She smiles grimly down at me. "I knew you weren't cut out for this family," she says.

A scream from behind us draws her attention to her husband and Krampus. She looks over her shoulder, but her hands stay locked around my neck.

I reach over to the bolt still sticking out of my arm. Fumble with fingers going numb until I find the metal head emerging from the back of my bicep, along with a couple inches of wooden shaft. I wrap my fingers around it and strain, but I'm growing weak with oxygen loss and the thing is fucking sturdy. My vision is starting to go black around the edges.

I summon every ounce of strength I can find, tighten my grip on the bolt, and *pull*. The blinding pain grants me a rush of adrenaline—and the shaft snaps in my hand.

As Louis's mother turns back to me, her face pale but her gaze full of determined hatred, I reach up and shove the broken crossbow bolt into the side of her neck.

CHAPTER

SEVENTEEN

Hot blood splatters over my face. Theodora gapes, choking out more blood, and releases my neck to reach for the wound. I shove her off me with a cry, yank the bolt out of her neck, and stab her again through the eye.

As I sit there panting in the snow—bloody, pained, victorious—I realize how quiet it is around me. There's no sound other than the gurgles of Louis's mother slowly dying. I turn to see Krampus standing, just as blood soaked as I am, over Louis's father.

The once-proud man is on his back, bloody gouges torn through his face and chest, gasping for air as he stares up at the monster towering over him.

"You... cannot do this," Louis's father gasps out, the words bubbling from bloody lips. "You... are... bound to our family."

"I am bound to our *pact*," Krampus snarls, his tail flicking. "A pact that your forefather made. We had a deal: I would reward goodness, not *cowardice*. Your family could have changed the world with the gifts I granted you.

93

Instead, you cheated my game and used your wealth in pursuit of worse sins. For *generations*, you have made a mockery of me. Glut yourself on wealth and pride."

He reaches down, wraps his metal chain tight around one of the man's arms. Louis's father fights, but there is not much strength left in him.

"No more," Krampus snarls. "Your greed ends here."

He pulls hard, twists, muscles straining. With a roar of effort, he yanks the chain and rips the arm off the man's body.

I squeeze my eyes shut and turn away, unable to stomach the screaming and the blood. I listen with a grimace to the clink of chain links and the subsequent shrieking as Krampus repeats the process with another arm.

The screams have gone silent by the time Krampus gets to Karl Kohler's legs, but he finishes his bloody work nonetheless. By the time silence falls, Krampus stands, blood-soaked with his chest heaving, over a corpse in pieces.

Between the two of us, we've turned the white snow into a battlefield of red.

When it's over, I struggle to my feet and yank what remains of the crossbow bolt out of my arm. Thankfully it went straight through the muscle, so while it hurts like hell, I can still use my arm. I lift my eyes to Krampus, who is staring at the body I left in the snow. His gaze snaps to mine. The look on his face is unreadable.

My own emotions are difficult for me to decipher, too. I've done a lot of terrible things in my life, but I've never killed someone before.

I'm a murderer.

It was self-defense, I tell myself. She was a horrible person. She deserved it.

None of that logic stops my hands from shaking.

I squeeze my eyes shut, trying to get a hold of myself. When I open them again, Krampus is in front of me. He presses a handful of snow against the wound in my arm. I hiss at the shocking cold but don't try to pull away. Part of me enjoys the pain. It chases away the confusing tangle of my feelings, and the thought running around and around in my head: *murderer, murderer, murderer*. The pain leaves no room to think or feel anything else.

I slowly lift my head to look at Krampus.

"Punish me," I whisper.

Absolve me.

Krampus doesn't look at me. He's focused on brushing the snow off my wound and replacing it with a bloody strip of cloth he winds around my bicep.

"We aren't done," he says.

That's right. Louis is still out there, because he ran, like he always does.

I study Krampus as he avoids my gaze. There's tension in his shoulders, and he's breathing hard. Mouth slightly open, chest rising and falling. When his red eyes finally shift to me, I see the hunger in his gaze. Killing Louis's father wasn't enough; he still craves more. He craves *me*.

It makes me shiver to be looked at like that. Scented. Hunted. The feeling that fills my chest is somewhere between terror and excitement, a dark thrill that ripples through my senses.

"You need it," I say, and it comes out soft and sultry. An invitation.

I need it too. I want him to chase away the dark thoughts that are threatening to overtake me. I *deserve* to be punished.

Krampus licks his lips, wordless.

I slowly reach up to shrug off my coat. My back still stings from the first whipping, but... "I can handle more."

It's an understatement. I crave it, perhaps just as much as Krampus does. I welcome the pain.

But he holds out a hand. "No."

I pause, my coat halfway off my shoulders. "No?"

He approaches me, step by slow step, his tail flicking behind me. "There are other methods of punishment."

Instinct urges me to shrink back, but I hold my chin high instead, facing him head-on. "Like what?"

Instead of answering, he grabs me around the waist and lifts me up. I gasp as my feet leave the ground, wriggling helplessly in his grasp. One of his huge hands spans my waist, and he carries me with ease, past the bodies of Louis's parents and back into the cabin. Away from where our final victim ran.

The warmth is a shock to my system.

"Where— What—" I can't seem to form a complete sentence.

He sits in one of the armchairs, his huge form barely fitting between the armrests. Then he arranges me on his lap, face down, bent over his knees. My dress rides up around my thighs.

It's so unexpected that it takes me a moment to realize his intent. My God. He's going to spank me.

The thought sends a bolt of heat straight through me. I suck in a sharp breath, and his huge palm cracks against my ass with a resounding *slap*.

"*Oh*," I gasp. Like the first strike with the rod, I feel more surprise than pain at first, adrenaline flooding my body and making every nerve tingle. I squirm on his lap, but one of his huge hands presses on my back and holds me effortlessly in place. Stretched out and helpless.

He smacks my ass again, and I whimper. Wet warmth gathers at the corners of my eyes—and the apex of my thighs.

"Please," I whisper.

He pauses. "Please what?" His voice is a low growl.

I reach back with one shaking hand and pull my dress up to my waist, exposing my lacy panties and the flesh of my ass to him. Krampus growls under his breath, the sound vibrating through his body. He shifts me on his lap, and through his loincloth, I feel the press of his length against my stomach. Fuck, he's *huge*, and hard as a rock.

Swallowing, I give in to temptation and reach for him, but he grabs my hand. His fingers easily encircle both of my wrists as he pins them behind my back and holds me in place.

"This is about punishment," he says, "not pleasure."

I lick my lips, daring. "I think we both know it can be both."

He grabs my thong and yanks it down. I gasp at the feeling of cool air against my bare and aching core. There's a pause, and I am certain he's noticed the wet spot on my panties, the shameful need.

Then he spanks me again. The slap of his huge palm against my naked ass makes me cry out. Then he does it again, and again, and again, each strike slightly harder than the last. Soon, I am gasping and teary-eyed and writhing. Wetter than I have ever been in my life.

"More," I sob out. "More, more."

He obliges. Between each slap of flesh, I hear his breath coming in short, hard bursts that tell me he is as affected by this as I am. The sharp sting of his slaps becomes a throbbing ache, my raw skin becoming more and more sensitive. But even as my pain crescendos, so too does my pleasure. I am drowning in twined sensations, raw and whimpering, vision going white around the edges.

Then, without warning, he stops. There is only the sound of my frantic panting. My body teeters on the verge of some precipice, stuck there. It is almost a worse agony, to be denied what I so crave.

"Touch me," I beg.

With incredible gentleness, he yanks my thong back up. Then he grabs my dress and smooths it over my ass, covering me. I hiss at the rub of fabric against raw skin— and whimper in disappointment as I realize that's all he intends to do to me.

"As I said, there are other methods of punishment."

He lifts me up, oh so gently, and sets me on my feet in front of him. I stand between his parted knees. He's so tall that we are face-to-face with me standing and him sitting.

My face is flushed and tear-stained, my need surely written all over my expression. My lower lip trembles.

"I need," I pant. "I need..."

He reaches out to me. The huge hand that just wrung such pain and pleasure from my body now caresses my face.

"I know exactly what you need, little sinner," he says. "But our work is not yet done." His hand slides down to grip my throat. "And neither is your punishment."

Then he stands, pushes me aside with one massive hand, and strides off. I have no choice but to follow, my legs wobbly beneath me and my core throbbing, wondering how much more of this *punishment* I can endure... and wondering if, in the end, that's all this is: the payment for my sins.

EIGHTEEN

K rampus and I head toward the forest in pursuit of our final prey. I pause to grab Theodora's fallen crossbow and quiver of bolts. I've never used one of these things before, but after a minute of fumbling, I manage to load it. I heft the weapon up on my shoulder, wincing as it jostles my wounded arm, and follow Krampus into the trees.

Louis's trail is easy to follow. He isn't a man who's used to struggle or fighting for his life; everything has been handed to him on a silver platter. As I follow the obvious markings—boot prints in the snow, trampled under-growth, broken branches—I imagine him stumbling through here, terrified and crying, and bite my lip.

I'm sure it's fucked up that the idea of my fiancé running for his life turns me on, but I'm past the point of caring right now.

On the rare occasion we lose the trail, Krampus pauses, sniffs the air, and leads us forward, following the smell of Louis's sins. His ears are up, his pupils wide, his tail flicking behind him. Just as eager as I am for the hunt. We move wordlessly, me with my crossbow and him with his chains.

I could distract Krampus, or try to slow him down. Delaying Louis's punishment in the hopes that the sun will rise before Krampus can give me my own. Now that I have blood on my hands, I doubt I'm going to survive the night. But... I can't bring myself to sabotage Krampus. I made a deal, and for once in my life, I want to be honest. I want to get what I deserve.

When I hear Louis swearing ahead, I hold up a hand, and Krampus hangs back. I creep forward on my own into the clearing.

Louis is leaning against a tree, sweating despite the cold, his frantic breathing forming clouds in the air and his legs shaking beneath him. It's clear he's reached the limits of his stamina. When I step on a frozen branch, the crack of it snaps through the air like a whip, and Louis whirls to face me with one raised hand.

The terror on his face shifts to relief when he sees me, but then goes wary again as he notes the crossbow in my grip.

"Diana," he says. "I... I was so worried about you."

I smile thinly without lowering the crossbow.

"What happened back there?" he asks, when it's clear I'm not answering. "With my... my parents, and..." He licks his lips and eyes the trees, as if merely speaking Krampus's name will summon him.

I cock my head to the side. "You didn't seem too concerned about any of us when you ran back there."

"What? No, I..." He shakes his head, eyes wide and pleading. God, he *is* beautiful, even after his run through the snowstorm. Maybe more beautiful than usual, with his cheeks reddened from the cold and his eyes glittering with deceptive tears. "I had to run! I didn't have a weapon, and I'm not..." He takes a step toward me. "I'm not strong like you. God, baby, I didn't realize how strong you are. But when the morning comes, we can forget all of this, alright? I can't wait to marry you, Diana."

As I study him, I think he might really mean it. Louis *is* the kind of person who would be willing to forget all of this. It's not like he's done anything to be proud of tonight either. With his family gone, he'd probably cling to me. This would become a distant memory, a night neither of us want to speak about. Maybe the trauma would bring us closer. Deepen our bond into something *real*. And with his parents and brother dead, I'm sure he's set to inherit a truly shocking amount of wealth.

I could live the rest of my life with him and be comfortable. Safe.

It's too bad tonight gave me a taste for something else.

"I'm going to make this fair," I say. "I'll give you a ten-second head start."

Louis stares at me, mouth slightly open. "Huh?"

"You do seem awfully fond of running, so I'll give you one last shot at it." I smile, taking aim with my crossbow, right at his face where it's frozen in that dumbfounded look. "Run."

He hesitates, searching my expression. "Diana..."

"Ten," I say.

"Please don't do this, I... I love..."

"Nine," I say.

He runs.

"Eight, seven, six, five, four..." I glance to the side, where Krampus emerges from the trees, his red eyes locked on the spot Louis disappeared. "Fuck it," I whisper, and take off after my fleeing fiancé.

CHAPTER

NINETEEN

There is something freeing about running through the forest, snow crunching under my boots, and knowing that for once I am the hunter instead of the hunted. I relish the sound of my prey crashing through the undergrowth ahead of me.

Krampus hangs back, following closely but not too close. He trusts me to catch our prey.

Louis may be a bit clumsy, but he's *fast*, his long legs eating up the distance much easier than mine, especially with the weight of the crossbow in my arms. But I know he isn't built for this. The man has never struggled or sweat or bled in his life. He doesn't have the grit that I do.

As I expect, he tires out first. His sprint slows to a jog, and then a walk, and then a stagger. When he trips over a snow-covered tree root, he struggles to get up again. And all the while, I am following him, slower but far more relentless.

And when he does get to his feet, he makes the mistake of heading for a clearing. Maybe he thinks it will help him run faster, but it also gives me a clear line of sight.

I stop at the tree line, lift my crossbow, and take aim. My numb fingers close around the trigger, and the bolt shoots out.

Louis falls to the snow with a cry, the bolt sticking out of his leg.

I grin, tossing the crossbow aside, and walk toward him. He writhes in the snow, wailing in surprise and pain.

"I've got him," I call.

When Louis sees Krampus emerge from the trees, he tries to crawl, dragging himself across the ground. But the monster plants a hoof right on Louis's lower back, pinning him in place.

"No," Louis gasps out, fingers scrabbling uselessly against the snow. "Please—"

Krampus grabs one of his arms and twists it. He clamps a shackle over Louis's wrist.

"No, no, no—"

Krampus flips him over with one hand and shackles his other wrist. They're bound in front of him now, and Louis is helpless and terrified in front of the monster. Krampus removes his hoof from his back, grabs the other side of the chain, and begins to walk, dragging Louis behind him.

I follow them deeper into the woods, smiling all the while.

Louis shrieks and cries as Krampus drags him through the snow. His boots kick uselessly against the ground. His weight doesn't even slow the huge monster down as he treks through the forest.

I follow a few paces behind. My stomach is in knots with both fear and anticipation. I've been waiting for this— dreading it, craving it, I don't even know anymore—all night. Krampus will decide what Louis deserves. Whether he will die here with the rest of his family or not.

And after that, I will be the only one left to be punished. My time is running out. Every time I think about it, the knot in my stomach winds tighter. It's a feeling of both terror and anticipation. Standing at the edge of a precipice again, and this time I'm going to let myself fall.

Deep within the woods, Krampus stops outside of the rocky entrance to a cave. But instead of taking us inside, he grabs Louis and drags him up to his knees in the snow. Then he rakes massive claws down his back, shredding his shirt and leaving his torso bare.

I slowly step forward until I'm standing right in front of Louis, with Krampus behind him. Louis looks up at me, his beautiful blue eyes filling with tears.

"Diana," he whispers. "Help me."

I reach down and cup the side of his face, watching a tear trek down over one cheekbone. Behind him, Krampus is lifting his birch rod.

"No," I say to Louis.

The rod comes down, slapping hard against my fiancé's exposed back. He cries out, tears flowing freely now.

Another crack of the rod. I keep my eyes locked on Louis's face, refusing to look away from him. I watch as he flinches and cries with every crack of wood across his skin. After a few hits, Krampus flicks blood off it, splattering red against the white snow. Krampus was really holding back with me. He has no such mercy for the man who betrayed me.

With every crack of the rod, my back stings with remembered pain, and heat slowly unfurls in my lower belly. It isn't just the triumph of well-deserved revenge.

There is something else, something wicked in me that delights in seeing his pain.

When Louis's eyes slide shut, I slap his cheek, and he opens them and refocuses on me. He's panting and gasping, his once-perfect face a mess of tears and snot.

"Why?" he asks, staring up at me.

I cradle his cheek. "You know why."

Krampus pauses, the rod drawn back in preparation for another blow. "Tell her."

"What?" Louis's lower lip trembles. "I don't, I'm not—"

Krampus hits him again, and he sobs into my palm.

"Confess your sins," Krampus orders. "Tell her why you deserve this."

"I don't," Louis cries. "I don't deserve—"

Another blow, and he cuts off in a cry of pain.

"I'm sorry," he gasps out finally. "I'm sorry, Diana. I'm sorry for bringing you here, for lying to you—"

"For letting your brother and father drag me to the door like an animal?" I press, my nails digging into his skin as I hold his gaze. "For being willing to let me die because your family said so?"

"Yes," he gasps, "All of it. You didn't deserve any of it."

I search his expression. Red-eyed and whimpering on his knees, his back flayed open by Krampus's rod, he looks like he means it. And it's surprisingly good to hear him say it.

I lean down and press a kiss to his forehead. His skin is hot beneath my lips. He shudders, leaning into my touch.

"I forgive you," I whisper, and pull back. Then I look over his shoulder and smile. "But it's not my decision, I'm afraid."

. . .

KRAMPUS DOESN'T STOP until Louis's eyes roll back in his head and his body slumps, limp in the snow. Blood paints the white around him and oozes from the gashes crisscrossing his back.

But when I kneel in the snow and lift his head by a handful of blond hair, he's still breathing. Just unconscious from more pain than he could handle.

Good. Those marks on his back aren't going to fade. I hope every time they twinge in remembered pain, he thinks of me.

I let Louis's head flop back down and look up at Krampus from where I'm crouched. He stands with his head back and his eyes shut. With his birch rod hanging loosely from his hand and snow falling on his face, he looks almost peaceful. But after a moment, his eyes slide open and fix on me. As our gazes lock, I'm sure we're both remembering that his work for the night isn't yet done.

He drops both the birch rod and the chains, and steps around Louis's limp body. My heart begins to race as he approaches. When he steps behind me, I rise to my feet but stay in place.

Both of his large hands settle on my waist, entirely encircling my torso. His hard chest presses into me, and a hot exhale ruffles my hair from above. I shiver, tilting my head back to look up at him.

"You enjoyed that," he says, like an accusation.

"Of course I did." I try to control my breathing as one of his hands slides over my stomach and down, down. "I told you from the start that I wanted revenge."

"That was not the only reason you enjoyed it." His hand slides down between my legs, cupping me. Palming the damning dampness between my legs. "Wicked woman," he murmurs, his mouth against my ear.

I press my ass into him, and a hard length meets me. I whimper.

"I'm not the only one who's wicked," I whisper. "You pretend to be above it all. To hand out justice for the sake of justice. But you do it because you like it." I grind back against him, drawing a deliciously low groan from his lips. "Because it turns you on."

"I never denied I was a monster," he says.

"I guess I'm a monster too."

He growls in response, two thick fingers sliding under my panties to rub over the wet heat of my core. I try to turn my head to meet his lips, but his other hand grabs me by the chin and jerks my face forward. He forces me to gaze down at the bleeding, unconscious body of my fiancé. The man we just tortured together. He makes me face just how messed up this situation is as he starts to fuck me slowly with his fingers.

"What a wicked little thing you are," he says, his voice a low growl.

I swallow hard. "Yes," I whisper. When I admit it, he lets me look up at him.

His eyes are black with lust as he gazes down at me. His nostrils flare as he breathes me in. He uses his grip on me to drag me closer, and leans down to press his nose into my neck, inhaling again. His hot breath sends goose bumps rippling all over my body, and I tilt my head back, surrendering my neck to him.

He growls again, and it vibrates through me.

"Your sin smells so sweet," he says, pulling back to meet my eyes. "I don't know if I will be able to hold back."

"Then don't try."

His lips peel back, revealing sharp teeth in an expression that's half snarl and half grin. "You've seen what happens when I don't."

He's right. I'm fully aware of what those teeth and claws can do, the massive strength he wields. He killed the family I was almost a part of. That should frighten me, but... it doesn't.

"I know you will give me exactly what I deserve," I say. "No more and no less."

TWENTY

Krampus studies my face. "You crave the punishment."

I feel naked under his gaze. I turn my face away, but his other hand grabs me by the chin and forces it back toward him.

"I need it," I whisper.

"Or what?"

"Or..." I shake my head. "I don't know."

He grips me harder in response. "Yes, you do. Why do you want to be punished?"

I shut my eyes, unsure what to say. The hand between my legs grips me harder, and I groan, lifting my hips. I want to grind against him, but he holds me too tightly, making it impossible to move.

"Why do you crave punishment?" he demands again. "Tell me."

"Because I deserve it," I burst out. My eyes fly open, and I look up at him. "Because it is the only way I can be forgiven."

"You think I am the one who needs to forgive you?"

"No," I admit. "But... I need to be punished to forgive myself." It's hard to voice it aloud, and tears gather in the corners of my eyes. I blink them away and gaze up at him, knowing my desperation is written all over my face. My mind flashes to Adrian's severed head, the crossbow bolt sinking into Theodora's neck, Karl's limbless body, Louis falling in the snow. All of my lies and deceit and thievery over the years. I *need* the cleansing pain that only Krampus can give me. I need to know if I deserve to live after all that I've done. "Please."

Krampus relinquishes his grip on my chin. A moment later, his hand retreats from between my legs as well, leaving me aching and unfulfilled. His tail swishes behind him, but the rest of him remains stonily still.

"Take off your clothes," he says.

I suck in a surprised breath. Glance at Louis, still unconscious on the ground beside us. Then I rush to unbutton my coat, fingers fumbling in their eagerness. I shrug off the bloodstained fabric and tug my dress over my head. Next, I unclasp my bra. My nipples harden in the sudden cold, and I feel Krampus's eyes on me. I toss the bra aside and then slowly reach down to discard my panties, the last thin barrier of clothing. I kick them to the side and stand in front of the massive monster utterly naked, vulnerable and shivering in the cold.

"Get on your knees."

I lower myself to the ground, wincing as my knees hit the biting chill of snow. For a moment, Krampus merely gazes at me there.

"Crawl to me," he says.

The demand floods my body with pure heat, chasing away the frost. I place my trembling hands in the snow and move toward him on my hands and knees. By the time I reach him, I'm shaking with both lust and cold. I sit back on my heels again, swallowing hard as I see the bulge of his arousal through the loincloth he still wears.

Sensing my gaze, he grabs the piece of fabric and rips it off of himself.

His length springs free, thick and dark and throbbing. I gasp in genuine shock. I imagined the size of him would be impressive, but *this* is beyond my expectations. He's so big, it sends a jolt of genuine fear through me.

He grins as if reading my thoughts. "Beg for your punishment, Diana."

Despite the fear racing through me, my lust rises to match it. I genuinely don't know if I can handle him, but I am determined to try.

I look up at him, making eye contact as I deliberately run my tongue over my lips. "Please," I say, my voice coming out half whimper. "Give me what I deserve."

His massive cock hardens more, right in front of my eyes. "Show me how badly you want it."

I shuffle forward on my knees and wrap my trembling hands around him. With both hands, I can just barely encircle his shaft. He lets out a growl low in his throat at my touch, and I suck in a small breath. He's hot and heavy in my palms, soft skin over steel-like hardness. I slowly run my hands over him, from base to tip, and then work my way back down. As precum gathers on his head, I rub my hands over it and then stroke him again, faster, with the slickness aiding the motion.

I lick my lips, gaze darting between the glorious length in front of me and his face looking down at me. There's no way I can fit this thing into my mouth without breaking my jaw, but God, I want a taste. I lean in and slide the flat of my tongue over his slit.

Krampus lets out a low grunt that sends heat throbbing between my legs. I release him with one hand, reaching down to touch myself, but he instantly grabs my wrist and jerks it back up.

"Have you forgotten this is a punishment?"

"S-sorry." I press my thighs together, trying to suppress the needy throbbing between them, and focus on working my hands over his length again.

He releases my wrist and cups the back of my head, pushing my face toward that massive cock.

"I... I can't..." I whisper.

"*Try*," he demands.

I take in a shaky breath and open my mouth as wide as I can. With my jaw straining, I manage to take in just the tip of him, swirling my tongue around his head.

Still, his hand urges me forward. Breathing hard through my nose, I lift myself up on my knees and force myself to take in more, more. Saliva pools in my mouth and tears spring to my eyes as I choke on him.

I've barely taken any of his massive cock, but Krampus rewards me with a moan that vibrates all the way down his length. My hands continue to work his shaft as I lick and suck at the sensitive head. Soon, spit is dribbling out of the corner of my mouth and down my chin, and I'm gasping and teary-eyed with the effort of pleasing him. I forget the sting of snow against my knees, my body laid bare in the cold. Everything but his cock filling my mouth and the greedy ache of my own need.

He pushes my head down again. I didn't think it was possible for him to go deeper into me, but he does, as my throat spasms and tears stream down my face. I can't move, can't breathe, can't do anything but take it as he slowly fucks my face. He holds me there for a second, two seconds, three, till the lack of oxygen starts to make my head spin, and then releases me and pulls out of my mouth with a wet *pop*.

I gasp for air, my face a mess of tears and spittle. He swipes a thumb under my eyes, licks it, and grunts in approval.

Then he grabs me around the waist with one massive hand and throws me over his shoulder. I yelp in surprise, and he gives me a firm smack on my bare ass for squirming. I'm still sore from my earlier spanking, so I whimper and lie there, dizzy and upside-down, as he carries me into the nearby cave.

I take one last glance back at Louis, lying unconscious and bloody in the snow.

CHAPTER

TWENTY-ONE

When we step inside the cave, it's surprisingly warm and dry, out of the howling wind of the storm. There's a circle of rocks where a fire must sit at times, with a metal spit and a large iron pot to cook with. A nest of animal pelts and furs sits in the back of the stone recess, atop a huge stone slab that resembles a bed. Is this where Krampus sleeps? His home?

It'd be cozy, if I weren't in the middle of a possibly fatal punishment.

Krampus brings me to the pile of furs and tosses me down onto the surprisingly soft surface.

He sinks to his knees between my spread thighs and grabs my ankles. As he pushes some of the furs aside, it reveals shackles built into the stone slab beneath.

My breath quickens. Is this a bed, or some kind of sacrificial altar?

Krampus clamps a shackle around each ankle, binding me, and then cuffs my wrists as well. I'm spread out in front of him, completely naked and exposed, unable to do anything but wriggle.

114

I brace myself for pain. But instead he bends down, lowering his head between my legs.

The first stroke of his long tongue makes me whimper. I'm so wet and achingly sensitive, I'm sure I'll come in seconds... except the moment I feel myself getting close, he draws back. Sits up so that I can see that tongue sliding over his teeth, tasting me and denying me. Then he lifts one huge hand and slaps my pussy.

I arch, gasping in shock and pain. He waits a couple of seconds and then bends down and licks me again, his tongue hot and muscular as it runs over my sensitive core.

Again he brings me right to the edge of an orgasm. Again he stops, and delivers a stinging slap to my sensitive flesh. I cry out this time, thrashing in vain against my restraints.

By the third slap, I'm sobbing, begging, tears running down my face as I plead for release.

I like being teased, but this is different. This is *torture*. He brings me so close to that delicious edge, but over and over again, he brings me back down before I can reach my peak. No matter how much I beg, he doesn't give in. When I get desperate enough to grind against his mouth, he clamps down on me with his big hands and holds me in place.

Soon, my whole body is shaking. My skin feels raw, so sensitive that even the sensation of his hot breath sends electricity zapping through me. I'm a whimpering mess, tears spilling down my cheeks, gasping for breath. My pussy is throbbing, clenched around nothing, dripping with evidence of how painfully turned on I am.

Krampus leans over me, studying my face.

"Please," I sob. "I can't take it. Please let me come."

"Mmm." His long tongue snakes out, licking the tears

off my cheeks, and even *that* makes me moan. "But do you deserve it?"

My mouth opens and shuts. My thoughts are too scattered for me to form a coherent thought. Krampus grabs my face when he sees my hesitation, long fingers digging into my cheeks.

"Tell me," he demands. "Do you deserve it?"

Does he mean the pain or the pleasure? I honestly don't know what my answer is to either one. "I... I deserve..." I focus on his red eyes, draw in a shaky breath. "I deserve whatever you want to give me."

He smiles. Releases my face. Then he lowers himself between my legs again and shoves his long tongue inside of me.

I break into a million pieces.

Toes curling, thighs shaking, eyes rolling. My vision goes white around the edges. I'm pretty sure I'm screaming, actually *screaming* with my release, but I can barely hear it. All I'm aware of is the pleasure crashing over me, stealing my breath, banishing every thought but *yes, yes, yes.*

Krampus keeps thrusting his tongue into me, and the pleasure keeps coming and coming and coming as my screams die down to helpless little mewls. Finally, I go limp.

But Krampus doesn't let up. His tongue recedes only to be replaced by his fingers. I tense for a moment, anticipating claws—but, thank God, they must be retractable. Thick, blunt fingers curl inside of me while he laps at my clit. I'm so overstimulated, it's almost painful, but he drags another orgasm out of me almost instantly, a brief but intense flare of heat making me shake and sob.

I'm throbbing, spent. But his fingers keep moving, his tongue keeps swirling around my clit. I writhe in my bindings, begging, trying to *escape* the sensation now. He holds me down and slides a third huge finger into me, stretching me out as his tongue continues its relentless pace against my sensitive clit. He forces me to come again. Harder than before, and I cry out with both pain and pleasure, my entire body spasming.

Krampus finally retracts his fingers, leaving me tingling and dazed. I'm limp as he removes the shackles from my ankles and wrists. I only stir when he clamps something around my neck. My eyes flutter open, blinking tears away, and I raise a hand to the metal collar.

TWENTY-TWO

Krampus holds the length of chain in one fist. A leash. He uses it to drag me up and then flip me over, positioning me on my hands and knees. My legs are so shaky they barely hold me, but he yanks on the chain to force my head to stay up.

He positions himself behind me on his knees. I gasp at the first brush of his cock's head against my entrance, but my body is still so wrung out and boneless that I'm not sure it's even possible for me to tense in fear.

And despite that flicker of nerves, I still want this. I begged him, and now he's giving it to me. There's nothing to do but take it like a good little slut. So I let my knees slide further apart and arch my back.

"Are you ready to take me?" he asks.

"Yes," I whisper.

My brain is so fried with pleasure already. He could split me in half with that huge length and I'd say *thank you*. And as the head of his cock sinks into my entrance, it feels like that just might be what happens.

Even though I'm dripping wet and ready for him, he

stretches me in a way I've never experienced. There's an immense pressure, enough pain to make tears spring to my eyes.

"I... I don't know if I can handle any more..."

He stops pushing. "You can take me," he says. "Breathe, little sinner."

I take one deep breath, and another.

"That's it," he murmurs, close to my ear. "Relax. Let me in."

My body slowly adjusts to his size, till the burn fades to dull pressure.

I can handle this, I tell myself. I *want* to handle this.

"There you are. You're taking me so well."

I'm still breathing hard, my body trembling. A thin sheen of perspiration clings to my skin. But after a moment I give an experimental roll of my hips, pressing back into him, spearing myself on his massive length. I moan, "More."

He delivers a swift slap to my ass, and I gasp as it stings already-tender flesh.

"You'll take what I give you," he rumbles. "Do not forget, you are still being punished."

I squeeze my eyes shut and force myself into silence. Inch by inch, he sinks into me. I am sure I can't possibly take more; it's not physically possible for me to take all of him. But then he shoves in another inch. And another.

He's going to break me. I'm shaking, gasping, fresh tears rolling down my face. It hurts so badly, and yet—

I want it. I crave it. I need it.

And once he's finally fully seated within me, I am full in a way I did not know was possible. My toes curl, my back arching. Pain and pleasure mingle in a dizzying cocktail. I want to beg him to fuck me, but instead I bite my tongue and let out only a whimper.

Krampus grunts in approval. That's all the warning I get before he pulls out and slams back into me in one quick thrust, his hips slamming against my bruised ass. I cry out, and his fingers dig into my skin as he begins to fuck me slow and hard.

It hurts. My body wasn't built to handle something this size. Each thrust is brutal, bruising. Forceful enough that only his ironlike grip on my waist is holding me in place. My trembling arms give out, and I fall face down on the makeshift bed.

Krampus continues to fuck me without pause, his massive body leaning over to pin me prone beneath him. My cheek presses against the furs so hard, I can feel the stone slab beneath. When I try to push myself up on my elbows, he shoves me back down with an inhuman snarl. I glance over my shoulder to see his red eyes are blazing, his long tongue hanging out as he pants with each thrust into me. He fucks me like an animal, wild and feral. He is all beast now, driven by his need and his desire to *punish*.

God help me. I love it.

Soon, I am gasping and writhing, my eyes rolling, my cries of pleasure echoing around the cavern. This punishment, this pleasure, fills some dark hole inside of me. It is everything I needed and never knew how to ask for.

If I survive this, I'll be ruined forever. How could I possibly be satisfied by a normal-sized man after being wrecked by him like this?

His grip on my waist tightens, and he lifts me fully off the bed. One huge hand holds me aloft as he settles back on his heels, thrusting up into me. I can't even move, can't do anything but cry out in pleasure and let him use my body like a toy.

"My little sinner," he growls. "You suffer so prettily for me."

Those words of praise send a throb of heat through me. I start to shake, on the verge of yet another orgasm that just might kill me.

His breathing grows harsh, his thrusts hard and choppy.

"That's it," he murmurs. "Once more. Come for me."

I am helpless to do anything but obey. As I clench around him, whimpering and exhausted, he groans and slams me down on his cock as he finishes too. His huge length pulses inside me as he thrusts his way through his climax, spilling his seed inside of me. When he lifts me off him, an obscene amount of cum gushes out of me and spills down my thighs.

My head is drooping, my whole body heavy and limp, every inch of me exhausted and sore in the very best way.

I groggily look back over my shoulder at Krampus. "Thank you," I whisper, and pass out.

CHAPTER

TWENTY-THREE

KRAMPUS

K rampus cradles the small human against his chest. Her face is slack, her swollen lips slightly parted, her body entirely limp. She's utterly exhausted. Spent in more ways than one.

"You took your punishment so well," he murmurs, brushing sweaty hair out of her face. She looks so peaceful in sleep. Krampus had hoped to take care of her in the aftermath, but she needs rest after all she's been through. He'll have to do it without waking her.

He leans in, nuzzling into her hair, and sniffs. She smells of sweat and dried blood and plenty of his own musky scent. But beneath all of that...

He sniffs again, and sighs in satisfaction. Her smell is clean and pure. Gone is the mouthwateringly sweet sin that tempted and tortured him all night.

He was not sure if it would be possible to cleanse it without killing her. With any other human, he would never have tried. He was so used to dealing out justice in blood and pain. But this one was... inspiring.

Enough so that he was willing to bend his own rules.

122

According to the game, those who evade him until sunrise receive a reward. Those who are caught receive only punishment. Diana did not escape from him. But... nor did he have to hunt her down. She came to him willingly. That was different than being *caught*.

He would have to see if the ancient magic agreed enough to follow his will. But for now, the sky is beginning to lighten. The barrier between worlds is beginning to harden again. As much as he wishes to keep this precious woman in his realm, he knows she wouldn't survive it.

So he carries her out of the cave. Past the bloody snow and the bodies, into the warm safety of the cabin. He runs the shower for her, and washes her slowly and carefully, running his fingers through her hair as the tangles soften. She murmurs and shifts in her sleep, but she does not awaken, both from her fatigue and a heady dose of magic with sunrise's approach.

When she is clean, Krampus follows her scent to find fresh clothes for her, dresses her and wraps her in a blanket, and sets her in front of the fireplace. Once he starts the fire, he's satisfied she will wake warm and rested. For a minute he watches her, reassuring himself that she is safe and whole, even after everything that the Kohlers—and Krampus himself—put her through.

Then he forces himself to his feet and leaves her behind to tie up the final loose end.

CHAPTER

TWENTY-FOUR

The warmth hits me first. I haven't been so cozy since I arrived at this cabin. Maybe for a while before that. I feel so safe and comfortable that I don't even want to open my eyes. I cuddle deeper into the blankets and breathe in the sweet, piney scent that clings to them.

Other details sink in piece by piece: the crackle of a fire nearby. The carpeted floor beneath me. It's far more comfortable than a floor should be, even though my body is starting to remember the aches and pains of the night—including a different kind of soreness between my legs.

My eyes fly open as I finally realize what that means. I sit up, blanket slipping from my shoulders, and look around.

I'm in the cabin. The Kohler cabin, I should say, though I'm the only one here right now, and I don't see or hear any sign of anyone else. I expected to be naked beneath the fallen blankets, but instead I'm dressed in the cozy plaid pajamas I brought for the trip. I reach up, groggily brushing hair out of my face, and dimly register that it's soft and clean, no longer tangled and full of sticks and God-knows-what-else. My skin is clean too. I don't feel the telltale stickiness of blood or the lingering remnants of sex between my thighs.

But when I sit back on my ankles, I wince at a throb of soreness in my ass. My back stings as the fabric of my pajamas slides over my welts. I still bear the marks of my wild night—both punishment and pleasure—which means it was all very *real.*

While I was unconscious, Krampus must have carried me here, and left me safe, clean, and warm in front of the fire.

I'm kind of sad I don't remember any of it.

"Points for good aftercare," I mumble to myself.

The sound of my voice reminds me just how quiet the rest of the cabin is. Even when I strain to listen, I don't hear anyone else talking or moving around.

I guess I shouldn't be surprised. If their punishments were as real as mine were, then most of the Kohlers are dead now. Which means I'm now left with the consequences.

Shit. I guess I'd better figure out how to deal with that.

I mumble a curse as I climb to my feet and stretch out my battered body. My muscles scream in protest as I shake off the stiffness and hobble out of the living room and down the hallway.

I sniff. I'm expecting the scent of drying blood, decay, or at least disinfectant. Instead, it smells like...

"Coffee?"

I follow my nose to the kitchen, where a fresh pot awaits me on the counter. I stare at the polished, fancy machine with its many buttons, utterly baffled at the thought of Krampus navigating it with his huge hands, before I remember it didn't even exist in his realm. It must have been on a timer.

I huff a laugh at myself and pour a nice, full mug. As expected, whatever coffee the Kohlers drink is good enough to taste great black. I wrap my fingers around the warm ceramic and wander over to the window—no longer covered in metal shutters—to gaze out at the snowy landscape. I can see the spot where Louis's parents died, but there are no bodies there, no blood marring the white snow. I stare at the spot a while, still, remembering the bolt in my hands, the gush of blood from Theodora's neck. I killed someone there. The reminder churns my stomach, but the guilt is less intense today. I've already been punished for my sins, and Krampus deemed me worthy enough to survive despite them.

My eyes shift to fresh tire tracks through the snow; Anna must have gotten out of here before I even woke up.

As I stand in front of the window and stare out at the snowy landscape, it looks like a picture-perfect Christmas morning. The mountain is truly beautiful when I'm gazing out from behind a window, nice and warm, instead of running for my life through the snow.

I bite my lip, thinking. Remembering the way the cars disappeared, it's clear that whatever happened last night transported all of us who were playing the game to... somewhere else. *Krampus's realm*, Louis called it at one point. Maybe the bodies stayed there, too. But that still leaves one problem for me.

A *thud* from somewhere in the cabin confirms my suspicions. Louis is here, somewhere.

I swallow past the lump in my throat. I don't want to see him, but I need to.

It's hard to locate the exact source of the sound, but I

have a suspicion, so I head to the lounge. Just like the rest of the house, there's no sign of the chaos that happened here last night. None of Krampus's spilled blood or the destruction he wrought. Even the record player is back in its normal spot, intact, after being smashed. When I start it up, it begins playing "O Holy Night" again.

I return to the desk and bend down to press the button hidden on the underside. The secret door behind the bookcase clicks open, and I follow a spiral staircase down into the panic room in the basement.

The space is small and plain compared to the rest of the house. The metal walls are lined with shelves stocked with necessities like canned food, water, and old-fashioned weaponry. My throat tightens at the sight of a crossbow, and I shift my gaze to the map of the area pinned to one wall.

Beside it, there's also a fucking Christmas tree. Beneath the pine tree with its colorful winking lights is my tied-up fiancé, bruised and bloodied, with a gag in his mouth and a garish red bow on the top of his head.

Louis whimpers when he sees me and stops struggling. The stillness of prey when it sees a predator.

I ignore him, and take my time poking around the panic room. It's downright cozy here, with bunk beds along one wall and a small bathroom attached. The Kohlers really were well-prepared. Just not quite prepared enough to deal with *me*.

On a table against one wall, I find the book that started all of this. I pause, staring at it before slowly approaching. But I no longer feel the strange pull I did last night. Still, I'm careful as I crack it open and start flipping through the pages. My eyes skim over the oldest entries, decades and decades of *Kohlers* marked in ink and sealed with blood, but

I slow as I reach fresher pages. Now that I know the truth, I pay particular attention to the names I don't recognize, scrawled alongside Louis and his family. Names that never appear again. Even after *Anna Kohler* shows up, there are others.

"I'm not the first one you did this to," I say, "am I, Louis?"

Not even close. I count them as I flip through pages. Five different women brought as sacrifices for Krampus.

My brow furrows. After my experience with Krampus, I find it difficult to believe that he would have killed those women over minor sins. Even I survived my encounter. How is it possible that Louis would have brought five women deserving death?

Then I remember a comment I overheard from Adrian: *"You've always been picky. Hardly ever bringing girls here, and even when you do, they never come back..."*

Picky, he said. Like it was Louis's choice.

I sit cross-legged in front of Louis and pull the gag out of his mouth.

"I—" he starts immediately.

"Shh." I press a finger to his lips, and he shuts up, his eyes wide. "I'm going to give you one chance to answer me honestly. How many girls did you bring here before me?"

He gawks at me as I remove my finger from his mouth. A swallow. His eyes dart to the ceiling as he thinks. "Five."

As I thought. "And what happened to them, Louis?"

His eyes flicker. He opens his mouth and then shuts it. "Krampus," he says.

"I know he didn't kill them," I say.

Louis lowers his head. "No. But he... he whipped them." He licks his lips. "I... I wanted someone better. Someone purer." His eyes flick up to me. "I thought that was you."

I smile without humor. He thought he was better than those women, but look at him now, beaten bloody in his own family's game. "Hilarious. But you haven't answered the question. What happened to them?"

He shifts. Looks away. "I would drive them home and cut ties. Our lawyers handled it if they tried to tell anyone what had happened. Not that anyone would believe them…"

So he left them with the scars and trauma. That sounds about right. But as a seasoned liar myself, I smell something off. "So all of them lived?"

He hesitates. "One of them…"

"One of them *what*, Louis? You know I can just leave you here to starve if I'm not satisfied by your answer, right? Nobody's going to come looking for you out here." I lower my voice, softening my expression. "I just want the truth. Then I'll let you go."

Louis shuts his eyes. "One of them froze to death. But I didn't kill her, I swear."

I remember how it felt when he dragged me into the snow. When his family locked the door. "You left her to die."

His silence is all the answer I need.

Something pricks my awareness. Why would Krampus let him live after doing something like that? He didn't hold back with the rest of Louis's family.

Unless… he left him for me to handle.

My lips twist into a bitter smile. I push to my feet, grab the book—fuck, this thing is heavy—and head for the exit.

"Wait!" Louis calls after me. "You said you'd let me go!"

"I lied," I say, and walk away without another glance back.

EPILOGUE
ONE YEAR LATER

As I walk up the snow-covered driveway of the mountain cabin, I think about all the ways my life has changed since that fateful night one year ago.

It's still hard to believe it was real. Sometimes it feels like some huge prank by the universe that's about to come crashing down on my head at any moment.

When I first drove away from that cabin—watching flames climb the walls in the rearview mirror—I expected to get caught right away. Surely someone would connect me to Louis Kohler and his family, and suspicion would fall on my head when their mountain retreat burned down.

But they never found bodies.

I guess Louis wasn't as open about our relationship as I thought, since hardly anyone seemed to even know he had been engaged at the time of his disappearance. The story about the disappearance of the Kohler family was all over the news. But most people seemed to think they had fled the country, especially when news broke about all manner of shady business deals the family had participated in.

Once the luck from Krampus's magic ran out, a *lot* about the family came to light very quickly. From suspicious foreign ties to tax evasion to the disappearances of multiple women associated with the family over the years.

But nothing that linked me to the fiasco.

After lying low for a while, I went back to what I do best: conning rich assholes out of their money.

I know I'm good at what I do. A natural liar, some might say. I've always worked hard *and* worked smart. But... I've never had as much success as within the last year. Perfect marks fall right into my lap, and my schemes always turn out perfectly. At first, I thought it was some good karma after taking care of the Kohlers. Soon, however, my suspicion grew into conviction that there was something else at play.

Something like magic. The same magic that had let the Kohlers get away with actual murder for years. *Krampus's* magic.

I didn't win his game, but he rewarded me anyway.

It's granted me a level of safety and security that I never knew was possible. I've tried to do some good deeds to feel deserving of it. I've sent anonymous money to the other women whose names I found in the Kohler family's book, though I know I could never compensate them enough for what they lived through. I even reached out to my parents, after years apart; we're going to spend Christmas together this year.

But first, I'm celebrating Krampusnacht on my own. I rented a cabin just for the weekend. It's cute and kitsch, nothing like the monstrosity of a bunker that I burned to the ground last year.

I may not smell as sweetly sinful as I did last year, but I've still been naughty enough that I'm excited for the chase. I spend my evening eating Chinese takeout and sipping hot cocoa, and as midnight approaches, I settle myself on the rug in front of the fireplace and take the huge leatherbound book out of my backpack. I spread the cracked and yellowed pages to a fresh sheet and pick up the pen.

I mark the page with only one name.

Diana Wilson

I don't even flinch as the pen takes my blood. I've suffered much worse punishments.

Afterward, I take a long, luxurious shower, wrap myself in a fluffy robe and nothing else, and settle down in front of the fireplace, just the way Krampus left me to wake up last year. I fall asleep to the crackle of the fire, already excited about what will await me when I open my eyes at midnight.

Krampusnacht is here, and I'm ready to play again.

Acknowledgments

Many thanks to:

My copy editor Claudette Cruz ("The Editing Sweetheart").

My cover designer, NSFSanti.

My beta readers: L&N, Illyria, Cipher, An_na_ra, and Unfair-Town-8728.

The Romance Author's Writing Group and Indie Authors Ascending Discords.

My family, my partner, and my friends.

And lastly: thank you, as always, my lovely readers!

ABOUT THE AUTHOR

Skyla Gray is a romance author fond of all things scary and steamy. When not writing, she can usually be found gaming, cooking, or binge-watching horror movies. She lives in Arizona with her partner and an absolute rascal of a dog.

Sign up for my newsletter for monthly updates and free bonus shorts!

skyla-gray.com

Also by Skyla Gray

Monster Research Facility:

The Nightmare's Kiss

The Revenant's Heart

The Imaginary Friend's Obsession

The Valentine Society:

An Acquired Taste

A Matter of Taste